Dead Man's Tale

G.A. Lisby

Order this book online at www.trafford.com
or email orders@trafford.com

Most Trafford titles are also available at major online book retailers.

Note for Librarians: A cataloguing record for this book is available from Library
and Archives Canada at www.collectionscanada.ca/amicus/index-e.html

Printed in the United States of America.

ISBN: 978-1-4269-0020-4 (sc)
ISBN: 978-1-4269-0388-5 (hc)
ISBN: 978-1-4269-0783-8 (e)

Trafford rev. 05/10/2012

 www.trafford.com

North America & international
toll-free: 1 888 232 4444 (USA & Canada)
phone: 250 383 6864 ♦ fax: 812 355 4082 ♦ email: info@trafford.com

Contents

Chapter 1

Howdy

Yea, yea, so what do you what to know? What? What? Speak up, I'm deef. Well I was born in nineteen fourteen, on the plains of South Dakota, in a bitty town of Gettysburg. You could blink and miss it. My first recollection of the devastation of the First World War was the Spanish Influenza. Yep, the horse and cart would collect the bodies every morning and stack'em up like fire wood. There were no funerals either, everybody was just too sick. My mother was never right after that. She up and died when I was ten years old, died right in my arms she did. So cold that winter was. You could not bury the dead till the ground thawed out some. I guess if you lived through that you had to be pretty tough. Everyone was up and drinking turpentine to kill it, I reckon that worked the best. You were fined if you spit in the street or did not carry a handkerchief. Can you imagine if they did that today?

After my mother died, my Pappy and me never really saw eye to eye. I mainly hung out with the Injuns who lived in town. I became good at card playing. My best skill has always been the memorization of two decks of cards. Course Pappy being the town attorney put quite a monkey wrench into things. Especially the day I won the pool hall at the ripe old age of sixteen. I never did finish school but I got as far as the eighth grade. School was rather a boring place for the likes of me. I always did figure my kids got their heads for math from my side of the family. By the time I won that pool hall, I was up to two packs of cigarettes a day and pack'n heat.

What? No, I never did like hard liquor, never could trust it. Rather, I could not trust myself with it. That never did stop me from running boot leg out of Canada during prohibition. I only did deal in the best, mighty fine stuff if I say so myself. That's what the boys wanted and I drove it down. It got to be a big operation. The boys out of Chicago always paid protection to the coppers and provided us with some thugs too. I never had any trouble during those times. I was a mighty fine driver, but I tended to get a mite edgy.

No, I never fought in the war. I was spending those years in the big house for attempted murder. The most peaceful time of my life, I might add. Three squares a day and you knew what was expected of you. The rules never changed. Sure beat my marriage. Personally, I would almost prefer the box to marriage. You call it solitary now; I spent two years in the box. I deserved it. I could not stand, or lay fully extended. It was more or less a hole in the ground with a grate of it. I even trained cockroaches to send messages to my friends. I guess nobody would really believe me unless they had to do it. I was in solitary for throwing boiling soap on a guard. I wanted to get out of the laundry and work on the chain gang. I can tell you from experience that was not a bright idea. I would not recommend it. After two years, I could never stand up straight. See my hump? I could never put on any weight either, but I am plenty good and wiry.

Take the year when they held up the Piggly Wiggly grocery store. They had everybody spread out on the floor as hostages. I was already in my sixties and had the brilliant luck to get through the door just as they had every one kissing the linoleum. They yelled at me to get down and join the others. Forget that. I just told them to shoot, I was already old and smoke cured. I ran down that aisle and threw cans after me. They fired off a few rounds and missed. I made it into the back room and slammed the door shut. I grabbed the phone and threw myself on the floor and called emergency. Thank god that door was bullet proof. They picked up every one of those punks. They thought they could scare me.

Now my Missus, that's what throws the fear of God in me. That is why I always keep my hair buzzed. I'd tell the barber to clip it close. That way she couldn't get a hold of it with a pair of pliers. See, if looks great for an old fart, don't it? Quite the rage now anyway. My Missus was the reason I never invested in a hearing aid. I spent my whole married life wishing I was deef. When it finally happened, none to soon I might add, I enjoyed some blessed peaceful moments.

I can't say I am an educated man, but seventeen years total in the big house did educate me. I learned I didn't want to return. I did read every book I could get my hands on. I still mostly do. Why, I can go into entire libraries and not find a single thing I have not read.

Now my Missus didn't read. She never had to. She got what she wanted by using her tongue and salvia. Just like any politician, I call them flannel mouths. You know, they create their own jobs. I saw many a politician when I parked cars down town at the Ballard's ramp. Many a night I would drive them home drunk and disheveled, sperm all down their pants. The next day they would never remember but they always had the balls to ask who I was voting for. There is little difference between some of them and a criminal, then again, maybe no difference at all. I'm low but not that low.

My foot is a little bum. When I was real young, I helped a missy get home from school in a blizzard. She never knew how close we were to dying. It was so bad; I could only lead the horses by feeling fence posts as a guide. Then, the first thing those damn horses did when they had half a chance was run over my foot with the cart. As if things weren't bad enough to begin with, there I was in the middle of Montana with a crushed foot and a half frozen kid. I walked the blizzard feeling those fence posts with a crushed foot. Never trust a horse.

Nah, now my foot doesn't hurt. When I turned fifty I had the bones removed. They couldn't give me any more trouble then. That doctor did a fine job. I was out of commission about six weeks. Things got a little tight. That's when the Catholic priest and his attorney paid us a visit one evening. They started putting the squeeze on my Missus since she wasn't keeping up with her weekly pledge. I actually thought maybe he had come by to se how I was holding up. I ain't Catholic but even that turned my stomach sour. I heard them threatening my wife in the kitchen in those low tones. I couldn't walk, but I lost no time lurching out of the bedroom. I did some fine work on them with my crutches just the same. I'm low but I would never take money from a poor family. My kids and us had been living on rice for weeks. We'd have cinnamon rice for breakfast, then tomato rice soup for lunch, with rice and Span for dinner. It never varied much.

My kids never complained. My kids, for the most part, are my joy. They always were. I just sit back and watch them still. They never cease to amaze me.

Come on outside. I need a cigarette and I'll tell you the tall tale of how I hooked up with that female some people call my wife.

Chapter 2

Wedding Bell Blues

Now as far as I am concerned every one has the right to be miserable, that's my motto. Marriage, it ought to give you a clue when you hear the word commitment (as in nut house), or the bonds of matrimony (as in ball and chain), but that is just my opinion and it doesn't count for much anyway.

Yep, I sure did, I met my match all right. I did more hard time in marriage than in the big house. I must admit that at least in the big house the rules do not change. I cannot say that about day-to-day life in my marriage. No sir. Besides, a piece of paper is no guarantee of anything. It will not make you faithful or loyal or nice. It will never change a snake from being anything other than a snake for that matter. I do not recommend it for the faint of heart. From my standpoint, it was comparable to kissing hell full on the lips.

It all started innocent enough for me. I hit the Twin Cities to get some distance. I found a job as a security guard of all things. Can you believe that? Slowly I made a few friends at night playing pool at a hall on the east side. I kept low to the ground and to pick up a few extra bucks, I started playing cards quietly. I ran into this big bunch of Pollack brothers and one by one, I made a fair income. I would just pick one a week to drain a bit of cash off, no great shakes. Now these were good Catholic boys from a big farm family, you know the type. Kids to be used for free farm help. They all worked like dogs, I'm sure of that. They all left the farm as soon as possible; some had been shot up in the war as paratroopers. I bet they preferred it to farm life. Between them, they could fix, make and rebuild just about anything. I think mainly because they spent quite a bit of time destroying things. They were pitiful at cards and it took them a grand while to figure this out. Little did I know they would have the last laugh.

The best I can reckon, they must have all started comparing notes. Then all the fingers started pointing at me.

Wham Bam. They have this great petite, last of the herd sister, one of a kind and just my type. Yep, I was framed, signed sealed and delivered. Next think you know, Miss Pollack pit bull is charging down the aisle, these husky brutes got me sandwiched between them, and they re dragging my scrawny behind to the altar.

That's it. That is my life, as I have known it. The poker iron gates of hell flew open and I was on the slippery slope and going fast. The celebration after dragged on for three days, maybe a week. Everyone had polkaed his or her way through all the band equipment. An accordion was in shreds. Everyone leaning on it to puke destroyed the wedding hall's fence. Many had broken ribs to show for that. Flames destroyed three cars. Kids had drunk their share of the beer by hiding under the tables. Granny was hospitalized after doing the splits and winding up going through the horse trough holding the back up beer. She only broke a leg. Kids had been slung out the windows and had not been returned. A whole wooden staircase went missing. On and on it went.

Of course, the police were called. Don't be so daft. They put in at least three appearances that I can recall. Let's face it, everyone picks their hill to die on and these were fine Irish lads. Not one of them were ready to go down at a regular garden-variety Pollack wedding. Oh yeah, they made an attempt and busted a few bottles of beer over a few heads. Big deal. They mainly just sat back in their squad cars, threw back a few beers, pointed, and laughed.

Now, for this privilege, I had spent months learning all about the fine art of Catholic civilization and beliefs, to say nothing of the cost this incurred. Added to that, I now was responsible for the carnage and decimation of approximately three city blocks. Flies would not land near the area. Some kids were still missing and presumed dead. Granny was in the hospital and running amuck. It was all my fault now as a Catholic and didn't I feel guilty?

There I stood on the threshold of my life. Thirty-seven years old, a serious ex con with seventeen years behind bars, I had never seen any thing like this, and the best was yet to come. This was the beginning of their revenge. This moment in time would last more than fifty years. Till death do you part, as they say.

Did I love her? No, she wasn't my type. I felt sorry for her many a time and I tried to please her so hard. Why didn't I back out? I tried but she threatened suicide. I just gave up at that point. I did not have the heart to walk through life with that on my shoulders as well as everything else.

Did I ever have a true love? Yes, I did. It was pathetic cowboy love. Star crossed, just like old Will would say. That's another story entirely and for a different night completely.

Chapter 3

Fire Bug

Okay. I'm going to say a few things that you might not like. If you don't like it you can take offense. Then you can take you fence and piss off .

I'm going to talk about being a father. That's right, being a father. It's all about action. Just because you might have a dick and balls does not make you a man, a husband or a father. I learned that as I went along you might say. Nothing really great is easy and I messed up many a time.

When I first "hit the wall" as you might say, my daughter had just been born. She was maybe six months old. I could not get enough of her. Of course, working three jobs I couldn't get enough of anything, mainly sleep. I can't really say she was beautiful. We called her peanut head. Kind off odd shaped head, you get the picture. She was a happy kid, a little on the quiet side. Sometimes she would look at you real strange like a bug or something. Some people thought she was daft but personally I never thought so. Looking back, I know she was in the trenches and trying to stay alive.

But I'm getting side tracked. So, as you have come to understand, I do like my cigarettes, and being continuously jack ass tired does not always mix well. By that time we had rented a small homey place off Randolph Street. It would have worked out right fine to stay there too, big back yard and all. Anyway, after work one afternoon, I was holding and playing with my baby girl, and I nearly fell asleep. So I put her into the crib next to the fire place in the living room. I curled up on the couch. The Missus was resting in the bedroom getting strength to nag me later. Life was good, I had a purpose.

Next thing I know, everything went black. Coffin black. Then screaming and sirens, my hair stood on end and I lit up and shot out of that house like a cannon. There, outside, stood my Missus whimpering. Now I really wake up and realize, where in the hell is my kid? By that time flames were at the windows. I ran back to the house and these six burly firemen were holding me back. I started yelling, "I got my kid in there." So one takes his axe and another follows and it's taking forever. I'm yelling and screaming. If anything happens to my kid, my life is really over.

Then after a decade more or less they come out. One of the big brutes is holding my baby in the crook of his arm. Poor bastard, he looked like he had personally met the devil. His eyes were watering with black streaks running down his face. I was crying too. My kid was all smudged up and still in her yellow sleeper. Her eyes were wide and she was sucking her thumb. She looked around like, "What is all this?" I opened my arms to take her and she did the damndest thing. She would not come to me or the Missus. She gave us that look like neither one of us was playing with a full deck. Now that cut like a knife. I couldn't blame her for that, but it did make me feel like the biggest heel on the planet. Even the fireman threw me a look like he could have dug my grave and kicked me in. I couldn't blame him for that either. I have the

9

greatest respect for those brave lads. It took her a couple of hours to finally come into my arms.

I tried to learn my lesson that day. I tried to be right careful after that. The Missus bought a fire proof bed. You could burn a hole right through it to the other side and look at the floor. Just once, maybe twice I lit the oven with a cigarette hanging off my lips, kicked me clean across the kitchen both times. That saved me from getting a hair cut and nose hairs plucked for a clean while too, but I wouldn't recommend it.

Later, when all three kids were bigger, we would take a Sunday drive out in the country to cool off or just get an ice cream in the city. I'd light up to relax. I mean I wasn't dozing or anything. Damn if I wouldn't flick those ashes right out the window. Then wouldn't they get sucked right into the back seat with the kids. But they were bigger then, like I said, and they could fend for themselves pretty good.

Still a couple of times I got derailed and wasn't paying attention. I thought the kids were having a territory war in the back. I kept screaming at the whole she bang to shut up as it was Sunday and all. I was just about ready to use my right hook, when I glanced in the rear view mirror.

Shit. The car was on fire. Smoke was everywhere. Bam, I hit the brakes and jumped the curb. All the doors flew open and everyone bails out and runs for cover. Here we go again. Firemen giving me the evil eye. At least I was in a different city. I did have a reputation in the Twin Cities already. Thank God I was a firm believer in insurance.

What I am trying to get at I'll spit out right now. What you do as a father can comeback to bite you in the ass. About seven years later we were all packed up in the car having a Sunday drive to cool off. We were all plowing away at ice cream cones. I thought to myself, I'll drive by the old house and see if it is still standing. I drove slowly past the house and back through the alley. Then my girl pipes up, "Daddy isn't that the house you burnt up?" Kids don't forget. You wished they did, but they don't. Ever.

Chapter 4

Walking On Broken Glass

There she is, my daughter. I guess if I had to describe her, I would portray her first and last as the keeper of secrets. Not just of our family either, everyone tells her the most outrageous stuff. But my first, she saw it all and took it in. Like they say, it is not just being a survivor that counts, but actually how well you thrive.

I am right proud of her. I told her so not so long ago, right after the love of her life died. That is why I am here right now. This is where I will be until it is finished and that is my secret. I know you will keep your trap shut.

I first figured out something was way wrong when I started smell a strange odor on my kids. They looked groggy and sickly. By that time, I had three kids in six years. More or less a decade had gone by. We had bought our own new cracker box house, a two bedroom just like everyone else. We tried to fit in with the Jones. I was working three jobs.

My six-year-old son brought me the chloroform bottle when I could not wake up my daughter. I had arrived home early from work and found the Missus gone. I thought Holy Hell; this is her baby sitter right here in this bottle. She had told me to get her some chloroform for her bug collection. How stupid of me. The kids were her bug collection!

I knew my Missus was frustrated; being a wife was not a high priority, let alone motherhood. Most of her sentences always started with I, me or my. I never thought she would go this far. When I looked the situation over, a bell went off in my head.

My daughter was always missing complete patches of hair, and she was often sick and bruised. My Missus complained she was slow and clumsy. She was far from that. My son showed me the hall closet with the electrical cord and the chair inside. In his small way, he showed how his sister had hid for him food, a flashlight, games and even a pee jar. If he wound up in there his sister could keep him alive. They even communicated through the basement ducting vents.

Then it dawned on me, the time we had just moved into the new house, my daughter was just five. I was in the basement cleaning up and my daughter was on the top of the stairs, so happy to see me after kindergarten. Her mother was standing behind her telling her to hurry up. Then just like that, she lay unconscious and missing her front teeth at the bottom of the stairs. I thought I saw a push.

It would take all my past experience, all my hard time, solitary, my mother's death and all the hard blizzards to get me through this. I had to pull out every strategy from my head to keep my kids alive. That day ended all sexual contact with the Missus. No more kids from the likes of that. I had to walk on broken glass and not let on. I had to be more than a father, I had to run this complete outfit and keep them alive. I had to keep myself alive.

Everything shifted. When the kids were in school, I worked. They had two hours with her in the morning. I enrolled them in classes after school. I met then after school and attended to them before my second job.

Saturday mornings I brought them with me to work. After, it was the science museum program so I could sleep a bit. Then we would head out to a movie or swimming, whatever it took. This worked out right fine for the Missus. She really did not want a husband in the flesh or the real work of having children. All she was interested in was the image. That was fine by me. I kept us out of the way and occupied.

Even Sundays I started taking the kids to church of all places. We had a code. If the Missus woke up early, we would pretend to sleep in and we would go later, or vice versa. My kids caught on quick.

I was worried about my daughter and I had to make some changes in the household arrangements. That or she would not survive. I could see it in her eyes; soon she would have no spirit left. It might already be too late. Could I think of a plan? Thank Christ I had paid attention to this or none of us would have gotten out alive. Little did I know my daughter would later save my life.

Chapter 5

Check Mate

Sure, you can go ahead and judge me. You can call me a jail bird, emotionally deranged, poor uneducated bastard. It's all true; I know it better than anyone. But all I ask, is, think about it.

I could have walked out of my marriage right there; lots of schmucks do it everyday. I could have filed for divorce, not that common back then, but let's face it people did do it.

I am a lot of things but one thing I am not is disloyal, and I loved my kids. Being a felon I would lose. The Missus had all the aces. Would she divorce me? Hardly, she had me declared mentally incompetent early on. Which, when you boiled it down meant she got all my hard earned money made out in her name. That is why I never had two cents to rub together but that is why her good little Catholic behind would not be going anywhere. Would she want to be a single Mom raising three kids on her own? Hell, no.

I worked out a plan like Eisenhower in World War Two. I told her I got fired from my weekend third job. I had another weeknight job lined up, parking cars at a large downtown garage. No more security guard. What that means was TIPS, cash in hand apart form my paycheck and, if I got lucky maybe some sleep.

Then I landed the day job I needed badly. Go ahead and laugh. I became laundry foreman for the county old folk's home. That meant I worked five a.m. till mid day during the week and Saturday mornings if needed. It paid well and had benefits so the Missus calmed down some what.

Most of all I could see my kid's mid day and I was home on the weekends. If all hell was breaking loose on the weekend, I could always take the kids with me in the morning.

Of course, I would rattle the cage every so often and threaten to walk right out of the state. That usually calmed her drama down for a month or so, even improved the grub a bit. Other times, I'd act completely derailed so it would take the heat off the kid's. Throw her off the scent, so to speak.

I also started moaning about not getting enough sleep. All three kids in one bedroom, you got to be out of your mind. That was my strategy to get my girl moved down to the basement.

Before you call me a bastard again, think about it. She would have a bed right by the furnace, and have privacy. I showed her the storm window. She could crawl out of it, and I put her bed right under it. That meant if all hell was breaking loose she could bail out in no time flat. I even oiled it so it made no sound.

Then too, she would have access to water. No need to bathe with her brothers twice a week under the Nazi water miser. No, it was far from perfect but it was the best I could do at the time. She could hear any approach on the stairs and take evasive action if needed. She could keep clean, warm and safe. She had plenty of hiding places for food and books. Granted, it didn't look much different than Auschwitz but that was her slice of heaven.

She took to it like a fly on a horse's behind. She became so ghost like you could practically see though her. I smuggled in books for her. Eventually two of those crazy Barbie dolls appeared. Her hair grew back. She became strong, quiet and resourceful. She had been loyal to me and her brothers. It was her turn.

Chapter 6

Fish Tails

Tonight all I am thinking about are fish. My mind has always been thinking on fish, even back then. If you took a good look at my heart you'd probably find it covered in scales. Passion is a good thing, it gives you hope, it takes your mind away . Passion gives you a vacation.

Fishing was perfect for me to pursue. The kids were getting older. We got out of the way of the "Warden" so to speak. The best thing was she was horrified by water, damn good luck for me. My number finally got called. Since one of her brothers drowned, all it took was an inch of water and her hair started standing on end.

Me and the kids would head out early. I had everything ready and planned out the best I could. We would hit it hard. I'd be so excited I even slept in my clothes to save time.

Those were the best days. There just is nothing like mother nature. The air was knife crisp, the stillness like glass. We had freedom right, left and center. Peace like a fine cup of coffee. Kids learn from nature.

We watched snapping turtles on the bottom of the lake; water was so clear back then. We'd quietly peak on moose enjoying breakfast, and heard their call. Sometimes we'd fish in the reeds for sonnies, my oldest boy learning all about motors. We could always go deep for my dream of a sturgeon. We'd hook into a big wall eyed pike or northern and enjoy some real drama.

Before you go shooting your mouth off, think about it. My kids learned peace, patience, the discipline of stillness and most importantly freedom. I'll be the first to admit I was living my life on my knees, but for my kids it was worth every minute.

Of course nature is a mother and it can be heaven or hell. It doesn't always play fair. Minnesota lakes have their own way of thinking to boot. Once on Lake Milac's a storm nearly killed us all. I had the kids hug the bottom of the boat and since the motor was swamped, the oars were my best friend. I paddled straight out of the mouth of hell that time. My hair started to stand straight up and I'm sure we came right close to getting nailed with lightening. I probably was for all the difference it made.

Another time ice fishing, I thought I put the axe through my daughter's foot. I nearly fainted. I didn't but I did slice though her boot, her shoe, and three layers of socks and right between her toes.DAMN!

If that wasn't bad enough, once I took her bridge fishing for sturgeon, I could see them right under the bridge. I got so excited I nearly had to change underwear. Sure enough, I cast off with the big heavy gear and snagged something. My daughter kept trying to get my attention, I was muttering about "damn kids" or some thing to that effect. Finally my daughter pulled on my leg and I glanced down. HOLY HELL! I looked down to see all twelve nasty barbed hooks sticking right on top of that kids head. How can a person snag his kid's head, what are the odds?

Looking back, it was worth it. All my kids still love nature, and they all out fish me. They too love the peace and quiet of it. Even the ice fishing is peaceful, especially if you rent a little ice shack with a couple of bunks on the ice. All that throws you is hearing the ice crack under you. We'd all throw our lines in the holes and catch up on some sleep. If a jingle bell went off on the top of the line we'd reel the fish in. I'd put on the coffee and fry up a king's meal of eggs and spam. Life was good. Like they say, born to fish, forced to work.

All right, for the finale I'll tell you a true whopper. I was on the Saint Croix River minding my own business. All my kids were grown. Alone, I was out for silver bass and had an odd line out for a sturgeon. I was lighting up a cigarette and scratching my head.

Bam! It hit. What a feeling. It took all the line, all my motor's gas and you guessed it, no oars. That damn fish had caught me and he was determined to take me out to Lake Superior with a vengeance. I debased myself and started yelling for help. After four hours of fighting and running out of cigarettes, I was able to beach it with help from another boat. Ninety pounds of sturgeon and full with eggs. I even sold the eggs and made good money. Nah, I don't even care if you believe me.

Chapter 7

Jock Straps

Yea, I have to admit my passion has always been fish. My kids spent many a day slapping my face with a wiggling fish getting my cigarette wet. Life was good. Kids under stress need to be strong. A strong body can help build a strong mind. That is how I made it through the box, I honed my body down. Fishing will not accomplish that, don't be so daft.

I needed a plan to keep my kids strong and busy after school, less friction. The city park was just two blocks away from the house. For two bits a lesson my girl was signed up for ballet, tap, jazz, tumbling and gymnastics. The boys were whipped into shape with baseball, football, basketball, trampoline and in bloody Nordic tradition, hockey. I loved seeing them sprout up. I never pushed and rarely watched. It was their job and they needed to do it. They got everything ready and packed the night before. If they screwed up, I bitched about wasting my investment in them.

My daughter had a hard time with the bike. I ran behind her many a mile trying to balance her and my cigarette hanging out of my mouth at the same time. How was I to know her balance was affected by Missus well placed blows? Swimming had her skittish too with my wife's tall tales. I plunked her in the YWCA and in no time flat, she was off swimming with her friends across entire lakes and back just for the hell of it.

In winter, I'd go out to the ice rink, right there at the park. Like the Pied Piper, all the kids were waiting for me to put on a show. I'd put on my figure skates. Don't look at me like that. I grew up with all girls and I was always scrawny to boot. I would pretend I could not do much. I'd rattle around, fall and scream like a real sissy. Just when all those kids started making fun, I start my routine. I would pick up the pace and skate fast and wide. I would double back and glide backward aiming right at some of them. I'd veer off at the last minute and take a swam leap and spin. I would come out of it and start the whole thing backwards double time. I usually ended in a big finale leaping into a snow bank just for the hell of it, when I was truly winded. Then all the kids would dig me out and we would make a big whip all holding hands and snake around that entire rink. The poor last sucker always wound up being flung into space.

Yea, maybe you can say as a man, I should have played hockey. Okay put your money where your mouth is. Remember I am not stupid and I was pushing fifty to boot. I never held back my sons though. They would come back all battered. Sometimes we would even be picking somebody else's teeth out of their thick skulls. That was fine for them, but it is not my style, I could rarely watch that blood bath. It made my bones ache.

Now tobogganing is another story, right after a snowstorm. What a treat. I was always on the look out for a new hill and out we would go. I would always have practice drills with the kids and practice yelling "brakes" to make sure they'd all throw out their legs good and fast. I didn't want any slackers. Thank Christ I did too.

One jackass cold day after a storm, we loaded up and headed out to one of the hills on a golf course. I had spied it out and had been licking my lips drooling to try it out. It looked perfectly fine from the front anyway. So we set out and trudged up there. I noticed some other slobs had gotten the jump on us and I could not let that happen. We made it to the top just after they had. I still thought we could beat them down. We got all busy but they started down a hair faster. I still knew we could out maneuver them. I packed my kids on, revved up, and took a flying leap on the back. Now the other's were taking the backside down. It was uncharted territory to me but the competition got the better of me and we were almost gaining on them when . . .

Bam, they flew out of sight and next thing you know their toboggan was split and flying though the air. Bodies were flying in space and one had landed clean in a lake and busted though the ice. "Brakes" I'm yelling. "Brakes". Thank God I hadn't raised any slackers. We narrowly slunk away from that one. I had to sit in the car with the heater on and thaw us out. We were all a bit dazed at how close we had come.

Tennis was for the summer. No one could ever beat me at tennis either. I could play a mean game. I learned in prison against all those prissy warden's sons getting ready to go off to college. They thought they had it made looking at my scrawny behind. It got me outside of that laundry and I could put on a fine show. I'd make it look like I was a real bumpkin and once all the betting money changed hands, I would pick up the pace and play it like a mean game of pool. I could put English spin on those balls so no one could anticipate where that ball would veer off to. I ran them all over the court and my pals made a fair bit of cash on those play offs.

I saved bowling for those rotten mid western days. You know the days when twenty or thirty tornados touch down in 24 hours.

All kinds of misfit kids would join us and a few were down right scary. You know the kind that smells like popcorn balls and rancid Italian sausage. Once, one of my daughter's friends let go on the back swing and we wound up running for cover.

My boys loved go-carts, we call them chugs. We threw them together with all the leftover junk in the garage. We'd drag them to the top of the hill on our block, jump on, and pick up some mighty fine steam. Usually right about then a wheel would fall off and I would be steering with my knuckles on the tar. I never really got used to seeing the bones of my knuckles but my kids got right used to bandaging me up pretty good.

Other bleak inside days we stooped to rubber band wars. How pathetic, right? But we were really good shots and we would use the furniture for protection and a few strays always landed some how on my Missus ass as she ran for cover. To those, we always gave a thumbs up and two points.

Sport always helps let off steam. It teaches playing fair and teamwork. Throw that together with coordination and fast thinking and you have skills that last a lifetime.

Chapter 8

Guerrilla Warfare

Now you can go ahead and talk about your kids schools and how prestigious they are. Go ahead and boast. It doesn't cut any ice with me unless they have got good old horse sense. Take a good look around at some of these mental midgets who run countries. They come from the best universities, so what! What good is all that education if you can't read a speech straight, let alone answer a question without spitting and sputtering. Some have been so paranoid they can't have their own men in the under their roof. Other leaders can't crawl out of a booze bottle if their life depended on it. What really makes my skin crawl is to let a man run a country who can't keep his barn door shut. How in the hell can you trust a man that does not have the self regulation to keep his zipper up?

Now, my kids needed horse sense. You know the kind when your ears prickle. No kid should have to live like mine but I taught them to anticipate the outcome. Their senses had to be razor sharp. They had to be able to smell the ozone of emotion before entering the house. I taught them to run without shoes as not to make a sound. I taught them slow shallow breathing to be able to go undetected. I taught them not to argue for the sake of hearing their own voice.

They watched as I was belittled at nearly every meal. They just watched and learned. I would just smile and give them a wink. Save your energy for when you really need it. My mouth did not open for a stupid reason, why waste good saliva.

I still had my shit meter ticking. I always had a line in the sand. The Missus always had a big toe right on that line. She always had problems with lines. I felt pity for her wasting so much time on minutia, nit picking every thing to death. Control. All I can say is, if you ever get messed up with a bully like my Missus, run the other way fast.

I knew I had been successful with horse sense one fine day when my Missus started in on my daughter. She was rambling on about her "peanut head" and her all around poor looks. My daughter was on Saturday morning ironing routine. She was just taking it and taking it. Then the Missus crossed my daughter's imaginary line in the sand. The shit meter went off when the Missus made the comment "You can't make a silk purse out of a sow's ear."

I saw that five year old brain pause. She laid that iron down on my Missus favorite blouse. She spoke up in her small voice clear and deliberate, "If I am a sow's ear, then, as my mother, you must be the sow." Right there my daughter was fighting with her verbal sword. She did it. She'd be all right. She put her hand on her hip and looked dead at the Missus till the blouse was smoking real nice. Oops, what a burn mark. The Missus lost that round right proper.

After that, ironing was right peaceful for my daughter. She got behind that board in the living room and the imaginary walls went up. She had peace right there in the middle of that war zone. No one wanted their clothes burnt up.

My Missus didn't give up though and proceeded to mix it up with her a good ten years later. My daughter was just ironing away. My Missus thought she had a captive audience for her drama. She was ranting on and on. I could see her through the window. She was pacing and yapping like a wild bull. Once again my daughter had enough. The Missus was railing on about wanting a divorce, and at that pivotal moment my daughter agreed with her.

Bam, that wild bull saw red and reared up and stampeded my daughter. Can you believe that? I made it into the house to see my daughter out cold with that ironing board on top of her. My wife had lept on it and was winding up to press her fist with that hot iron on to my kid. Jesus.

My kid came around right quick and shook her self awake. Then she pulled in her arms and legs and bench pressed that Tasmanian devil right off her and across the living room. I just stood there dumb founded; my jaw was on the floor. I was seeing this with my own eyes. The Missus wasted no time and grabbed her trusty leather belt. She wound up and hit a homer with the buckle across my kids head. Before I could step in, my daughter took the second blow full force with her arm and clenched her fist around it and jerked it clean out of that devil's grip.

My daughter threw me a glance and I backed off. She wound that belt around her fist in the same tone as the Missus. She stood straight and tall. She walked right into the Missus space and met her eye to eye. In a clear voice she stated, "This is the last time. No more of this for me do you understand? No more! Ever." The Missus was wild eyed. She was backing up. She was shrinking right before all of us. Like the wicked witch of the west.

My daughter turned on her heel and marched out the kitchen door, slamming it behind her. I crossed my arms and surveyed the damage shaking my head. Holy Hell! I threw the Missus and evil look, and followed my daughter outside. I took a seat next to her on the out door swing. The boys stayed real quiet at my side.

We didn't speak. What could I say? I just peeked at the trickle of blood running down her ear. The scars on that kid's head must have looked like a road map. Her left arm still had the imprint of the buckle. After a couple of hours our breathing slowed and the mood wore off. I glanced at her full on and she looked me right in the eye too. Our stomachs were rumbling and I put out the invite of a nice burger and a turtle sundae to celebrate. Of we went, with the boys in tow. We left Dragon Lady in her lair.

Years later about twenty, more or less my Missus got her balls up and tried her last time to mix it up with my daughter. That's when the Missus entered her prison walls for good. But that's another story.

Chapter 9

Pay Check

See this photograph, yep that's me sitting right next to Ronald Mac Donald. Don't be so daft, of course that's a cigarette hanging out of my mouth. I got news for you, that old Ronald smokes too. I'm wearing my favorite hat, the one my daughter bought just for me; see is says "Old Fart". I worked there after I retired just to get away from the Missus.

I retired from working at the county old folk's home. What I learned in prison landed me the job, can you believe that? All I ever wanted was to work on the chain gang, and here I was again in another hot wet basement. I can't complain, it paid well and the ancient foreman was ready to retire. At least the place had windows near the ceiling all around. Those windows came in right handy to watch the comings and goings on.

Soon, the old boss retired and I was made foreman, not unusual back then as I was the only man in the outfit. I was the youngest at forty two and none of us were spring chickens. Once in a while I could find a male helper but they wouldn't last long, it was just too hard and boring of work for most men. I didn't lose any time making changes in the way it was run either. I wouldn't be sitting with my feet up. I already had a plan. The job was dirty, boring and heavy.

My plan worked well. I arrived an hour early, before the girls, at five a.m. I pulled all that heavy disgusting laundry from the chutes and sorted. I would not let the girls do this any longer, it was just too much. You can imagine. I didn't want to find any one of them on their back, dead like a cockroach with their legs up in the air on my watch.

I showered before the girls came in. I made sure there was no bickering. All of us paired up and rotated positions every two hours, no pecking order with me. There were two hours on wash, two hours on mangle, two hours on fold and sort. We took a small coffee break every two hours. By lunch time we had six hours under our belts. Think about it, all our feet and legs were wet, and on hard cement all day. All our veins were shot, this was no beauty pageant. But after lunch, I made sure we had down time. That's when we went on the sewing machines and mended, sitting down.

We worked like a well oiled Chinese parade dragon. We paced ourselves, if things were slower we worked slower, but usually on Mondays it was always a devil. I also fought hard to get the union in, and I did. I'm not crazy about unions but we needed any type of job security we could get, especially retirement for those old broads. I have to admit looking back; those were some really peaceful days for the most part. Everyone knew what was expected and did it.

No, I never had sex with any one of those old birds. I "never shit where I eat" as the saying goes. The big boss upstairs did not share my sentiments in that department. That was not any of my business, till Old Bess went to deliver his prissy starched shirts and caught him in the act with one of the nurses who had a hard time keeping her legs closed. This was an explicit tragedy for Old Bess, being an old maid and all. She came back all whimpering and upset. We stashed her in a huge wooden closet to calm down in case the big boss came sniffing around.

Sure enough, one of the nurses who was not real fond of him called and said he was on his way down. We got ready for action. We all got busy and I told the girls to keep their backs to him. I kept a real poker face. Just when he was winding up, I let go of the big machine's wash cycle and flooded the floor with hot soapy water and it didn't do much for his wing tip Florshiems. Then I went in to distraction mode and started crabbing about the drains. He promptly turned on his heel and marched out. I knew this wasn't the last of it.

He came snorting and sniffing around in the next few months. I was almost always tipped off from the nurses upstairs. We knew he was out for blood. He wanted the end of Old Bess, just to prove he could do it. Old Bess had worked there forever, she was just a simple creature and had never married. Now, I ask you, why would your pick on somebody like that? He was a bully, a mean bastard. You know the kind, the ones that get promoted.

I did not sit on my haunches, I did my homework. I had plenty of contacts with attorneys on my night job parking fancy cars downtown. I chose one with a long fuse and told him the shake down that was going on. He told me to keep my head down and my mouth shut, just to act stupid like. He'd look into things from his end, and to give him a heads up if needed and he'd come down. He gave me his personal number. I also had a confab with the union rep who was just a lazy mob plant. His job was to keep status quo so they could continue to skim off our backs. He didn't need to be in the way of shit rolling down hill either.

When it happened, it started usual enough. I got the call to go upstairs to see the big boss. I got Minnie to put the call through to the attorney and union man. I headed upstairs with one of the other girls as a witness. This did not sit well with him, I saw the scowl. I also saw the profile of the nurse with the leg problem listening by the door. He informed me Bess had to go, too old, shoty sorting. I kept low like Mr. Dumb. I politely replied that he would have to give me an example of her sorting mistakes. He huffed his way to the basement and we followed. I was buying time. Eyeballs were on us everywhere. The scent of a lynching was in the air.

He tried to show me a sorting mistake saying a shirt was in the wrong slot. I claimed the mistake and said he'd have to fire me. We bantered back and forth and I finally saw a car park in a stall right by the entrance. The attorney had arrived. A call came through that the boss was wanted upstairs. He turned and headed back up; informing me this was not the end of it. We all took a deep breath, then looked at the clock, count down.

I got the call and headed up. My veins in my head were pulsing and I marched up there. I entered the office and the shit hit the fan. The girls said they could hear me yelling all the way to the basement. It went on and on. The union rep chimed in and got things really convoluted. I was still ranting when four or five orderlies carried me back down stairs. That was about the closest I've come to a straight jacket.

I sat in the sewing room with the rest of the girls and sipped a coffee to calm down. They had never seen me explode before so they were a little rattled. We must have all looked ready for the guillotine. Our little tea party was over. Old Bessie was still whimpering. All we needed was someone to throw a casket in the room, a perfect funeral.

Chapter 10

Pay Dirt

Now, do I have to say it again? Rule, you don't shit where you eat. A lot of people do have sex at work. Fine. I believe it is a down right lazy man or woman that does. Either way you open up a real can of worms if you do. It's always been a personal code for me. Sooner or later it comes back to bite you on the ass. It's your funeral.

Like I said there we were all sitting at work in the mending room. Just like a funeral. Nice foul mood hanging in the air. Old Bess simpering away like someone had just ran over her cat.

Then Minnie our scrawny point man gave me a look from her position by the wooden doors. Okay, here she blows!

That slimy union man slithered towards Old Bess. She just covered her face with her hands. He started convoluting around. He always needed a translator. What it boiled down to was this; Old Bessie was getting a two week paid vacation.

Finally I kicked the box out from under him and got to the point. She had a rough time understanding she as not fired. The union man peeled off five one hundred dollar bills and told her to go get a manicure. Can you believe that? I'm sure that was money that he bilked off our backs but at least it was coming back around.

It took Old Bess quite a while to simmer down. Then Minnie shot me another look from the doors. Quiet as a raven's wing, in walked the long fused attorney, he motioned for me. I led him into a quiet area of the laundry.

He asked if I still had his personal number. I told him I sure did. He told me now was the time to keep a personal record of the big boss's comings and goings. I knew Minnie would relish this job. He also stated that more shit was on its way down hill, and if I became privy to any other meandering going on up stairs to keep him well informed. O yes, and to keep my head down and mouth shut, in other words, no more explosions. Then he quietly extended his hand and thanked me for taking care of his daughter last summer. He turned and left. At the door he glanced back at me shook his head and smiled.

I scratched my head and vaguely remembered putting in a young rich drunk girl in a cab and sending her back to her mother's. It was late at night; they thought they were out of sight in the parking ramp. I really remembered prying her away from her inebriated date by giving him a nice right hook though the car's open window. He never saw that one coming. Trust me, he wouldn't remember a thing. No tipsy young lady as going to get pawed up and possibly pregnant on my watch, especially by the likes of him. It never dawned on me that she might have been my attorney's daughter.

Whew, that was that! It was over, done. The home run was hit but the game was far from over. I went back to the mending room. I could have hugged and danced with each one of those old broads. They all had broad mainly toothless smiles for me.

I explained how we had won one round but only one. We had to stick together. Minnie relished the idea of being point man and recording the big boss's comings and goings. Everyone would keep low to the ground and ears open. No one would do anything alone. Any deliveries upstairs would be made in pairs. I had to keep scarce and keep the heat off. Last but not least, loose lips sink ships.

If the boss was spotted on his way down, I was to be given a signal. This would enable me to beat it to one of the chute rooms. and sort. No one was to go to the lunch room to eat, we didn't need any other ticking time bombs, at least till things died down. If anyone was to ask, we were swamped and a machine down.

This started a new routine for us. Good Old Bess couldn't keep a smile off her face. A two week vacation did no good for that old girl. It was paradise for us. She started cooking lunches with a debut of her fine ham hocks and beans, corn casserole and blueberry pie. She must have spent every cent of that five hundred dollars on those lunches. I was in paradise.

When you look back, we were probably the only real family Old Bess ever had. About ten years later she finally kicked the bucket. That same long fused attorney called me up to his office and informed me Old Bess's insurance was made out to me. I told him I could never take that money home. I'd never see it, it wasn't rightly mine anyway. He took me across the street and cashed that check, handed me ten thousand dollars in one hundred dollar bills. I sweat that entire night.

Next day, I called a work meeting and closed those mending room doors. I slapped a stern look on my face to get their attention. I said that there had been a lot of complaints lately. I handed each of them an envelope. Then I stated that one person who had no complaints was good Old Bess and she wasn't complaining one bit.

Chapter 11

Pay Back

Now, do I have to tell you again. Work is a good remedy for many ailments, for instance the me, myself and I complex. To name another, work is a remedy for insomnia. It gives you an outlet and helps to refine your personality. It's basic and important to teach your children how to work. It's the parent's job and no one else can teach this. Even mother birds make their nests tight to help their babies to fly.

Of course, I worked at doing a lot of things but even at home I had time to teach my children. You might think a man like me couldn't teach much and you may be right. I still kept those kids close at whatever I was doing, especially my two boys. All of us fixed the car and all the bikes We oiled, greased, swept, raked and washed. We all knew hex heads, washer bolts, box wrenches and ball peen hammers. My kids wanted to be with me, it was no bother to teach and explain things. Just like Tom Sawyer, I made it interesting.

As time went by, my job in the old folk's home simmered down. After the big fiasco with Old Bess the shit changed direction and started rolling uphill toward the big boss. Our little bunch in the lowly laundry came to find out quite a lot. The Boss was having relations with more than just that one nurse and he happened to promote those bimbos over the other staff with more experience and seniority. Those nurses had a big axe to grind and it was ready to fall between the big Boss's legs.

Funny thing, once everyone else realized our little operation in the laundry had stymied the big Boss, they all wanted to jump on the band wagon. Yep, the vultures stared circling. The nurses didn't want to be outdone by the mere laundry crew, how humiliating was that!

Soon, those nurses had circled their wagons and prepared their own strategy. One even snuck down and contacted our point man Minnie; she wanted the phone number of the slow fused attorney. You could smell blood in the air, and the gossip went red hot. I told my crew to lay low to the ground. When the shit was going to hit the fan, I didn't want any one of us in the middle.

Thanks to Minnie, we all started paying attention to the Boss's comings and goings. We even knew who else was with him. Minnie shimmied up between the wall and the mangle, she'd look up through those windows to report who came and went. She recorded everything. Before long, all of us knew who drove what cars.

I regretted having to return to the lunch room to eat. My crew could cook mighty fine and took turns putting out a fine spread. I really did appreciate it too. But we could not stay in the fox hole forever. Before this incident we were all but invisible, now our motley crew stood out like a sore thumb. So we got back on the horse so to speak and made our way to the lunch room. It wasn't too long before one of the Boss's weasels shimmied up to Minnie of all people. Damn, I hate a male gossip, is there any thing lower?

It took me a while to rattle my brain in how to shake him off. I just happened to know his weakness.

He finally got the nerve to slither and sit next to me a few days later. I was prepared. I had soaked a Baby Ruth candy bar in coffee and smeared it on my forearm. I knew he had a sensitive stomach, you see. I pulled up my sleeve slowly and sipped my coffee. He looked at my arm and asked me what it was. I matter of factly smelled it and stated it must be a bit of shit from the chute.

Glory be! He stood straight up and vomited over our entire table. He managed to clear out the whole lunch room. People were running in quite a panic. Funny thing after that, he never wanted to sit next to me. So sad! I even feigned waving him over. I wasn't offended, no one wanted to sit next to him and risk a repeat performance. We all barely made it back to the laundry in one piece after that one. I thought Old Bess would have to change her underwear, she was laughing so hard. Every once in awhile she would started chuckling and we'd all bust up. It was right fine to see her laugh for once.

Not long after, Minnie's book was requested by the slow fused attorney. The shit hit the fan. The Big Boss was indicted for his carrying on. Some one must have tipped off his wife because she started make surprise appearances, something she never aspired to before. Rumor had it he was skimming the old people too, taking part of their allowances. I had suspected this. The stew was begging to boil.

Then one day I opened the newspaper and it was all there. Like I said, you don't shit where you eat. Now he had his pants down and he was fully exposed. His days were numbered, and he was escorted off the property in hand cuffs. Not a pleasant picture.

You never know when a new boss takes over. Basically, you just exchange one snake for another. But you knew the old snake. Our new boss never carried on like the old one. Then again, by that time, we had a reputation. He side stepped the laundry as much as possible which was fine by me. He generally left us alone. He even threw us a few bones. We got new rubber mats for the cement floors. Nice fans arrived in the spring and the drains were regularly maintained. I was able to take the kids with me when it was necessary and no one ever said a thing.

I stayed till I retired. Can you believe that? Our crew was like a family, a good family. We respected each other. I enjoyed them all.

Chapter 12

Packing Light

Now, every year our happy family would try to take a vacation. I do recommend it. Yet, looking back on our "home sweet home" you can just imagine our vacations. In our circumstances we could have well used some down time from each other.

Oh, I'm not belly aching or anything, but think about it. Minnesota is a beautiful state if you don't live in it. On a year around basis it can made you a might edgy if not bring you to your knees. It's my opinion that the best serial killers come from that Bermuda Triangle of the north. There are all those white boys locked in hibernation with their mothers during the frozen six months of winter. That can be a real lethal soup. Go figure, they even had a jean called "Tough Mother's". The bill board advertisement showed a mean old broad exposing a firm bicep with a tattoo that reads "born to nag". Under those circumstances a vacation from your family should be a law.

A couple of times I got real frivolous and rented a travel trailer and crammed enough in it to pack the coliseum, and off we would go. The youngest was always a handful any way you look at it.

Any time he would get near a car within the first hour, he would be vomiting in the back seat. Then the Missus would look at it and do the same thing in the front seat. Ain't I lucky? So, that was how we always started out Then into the second day we would even get luckier and some old fart would end up hitting us and we'd be holed up in some god forsaken town in South Dakota. There we would all sit, eating jellified canned ham sandwiches at the sweltering mechanic's shop.

The send or third time out like this I finally rented a car. I left everything at the mechanic's shop. Finally we made it to Mount Rushmore just before sunset. We reached the lava beds around midnight and all piled out and took a look. We got to see Old Faithful too, but forty five minutes to see her blow was asking a lot. Heading back home, I got right smart and put the Missus in the back seat with the youngest so they could take turns throwing up. I kept my daughter and oldest boy up front with me. I gave them a wink and kept the windows rolled down and we were just fine.

Once and awhile I had a grandiose plan of renting a lake cabin. I would have loved to own one but looking back it was for the best. As usual, my luck would run out. One year there were May flies as big as bats. Every time you would step outside they would stick to you. How in the hell can you catch a fish when they are full of those giant May flies? It didn't stop me though. I stayed out in the boat and pretended to fish anyway. I could see my Missus eyeballing me from the shore.

Then the weather bogged in, it started raining dog hard, which meant all the insects wanted to get into the cabin with us. Just to kill some time, I sat and counted the insect bites on my oldest boy and when it got over two hundred, I stopped. Christ, here I was in vacation hell and paying for the privilege. I packed it in and waved the white flag and got the hell out.

Oh, sure I still had the vacation blues from time to time. My Missus swore off all vacations after the May fly incident and it worked to my advantage.

One year I took my daughter and oldest boy way up in Canada to a lake I can't pronounce. It was so beautiful, I just wanted to stare and scratch my head. We parked the car by the country store and loaded up a rental canoe. We camped clean on the other side of the lake. Everyday we explored the land and fished. We found shallow channels that connected to other lakes and we paddled all of them. That was the most outstanding trip for just the peace *a*nd quiet.

There were a few draw backs, Canadian mosquitoes for one. So you'd have to do your business fast or you'd be itching your behind quite awhile. My camp cooking usually ended in flames so my daughter tried to keep an eyeball on me. All of us hunkered down and caught up on some long last sleep, there was no one vacuuming at three in the morning. My daughter found a warm channel and we even were able to swim in those golden waters. We even kept spanking clean in the middle of the wilderness. We managed to stay the full two weeks till we packed it in.

Now don't you know, I got right cocky with myself. We had made it with all our supplies in the canoe all most to shore. Then I decided to stand up like a demented King Kong. I told my kids to hop out and I threw them the rope. Yep, I told them to pull me and the canoe with all the junk in. They looked at each other and then back at me and refused. They were not stupid. Then I up and yelled again "pull", so they looked at each other, and shrugged and did as I had so impolitely requested.

Bam, out I flew, over went the canoe and we had all the gear in the drink. I came up all blue ass cold. The kids were backing up. Then I did a survey of the disaster, I saw the toilet paper roll unrolling under the water, along with the camp stove. I couldn't help but start laughing. In the end it saved us from packing it back in the car. We celebrated with an ice cream at the country store and meandered our way back home.

I could have bought my kids a bunch of worthless toys but in the finish it's really these memories that you want to make. Nothing can compare to Mother Nature. These memories are the things you take with you that don't end up in the garbage in a few years.

Chapter 13

Pennies from Heaven

Bullies, it's almost like I was surrounded by them. How do we let them get so strong? Take for instance Hitler, why didn't one of those dizzy broads of his put some poison in his ear early on like good old Shakespeare would have done? How do these nut balls get the power? Is it just to hone the rest of us down? As far as my wife was concerned, like most bullies she had no life of her own. She was mainly always in good form to trying to control and make us at least more miserable than she thought she was. One thing about it, after the smoke cleared, I have to admit she made a man out of me.

Nothing compared to a hill of beans when compared to what she dished out. She denutted me like no one else. Not even the hard prison time could compare, but at the end of the day she could not come close to touching who I was. She was just another warden as far as I was concerned, a warden who changed the rules everyday. Like I said, she would switch strategy left right and center, but I got over it.

It was hard on my kids looking back but I was the perfect match for the Missus darkness. Money was always a high priority for her. She tired to control it too. She had me declared legally incompetent early on and my every paycheck was made out into her name. What the hell she ever did with the money is a good question. Money never meant much to me.

As far as me and the kinds, money doesn't count for actual presence and I was with them as much as possible. I taught them what I could about money, and what I did not know I tried to find other people who could. Old maid Bess had shown my daughter how to crochet, and knit and helped with her sewing on Saturday. Bess was so proud. Then, where I worked, when a person kicked the bucket, I'd take my daughter over before the clothes were donated and see if she could remake anything to fit herself or the boys. Mainly with those Minnesota winters some of those coats came in handy. We'd all pick them apart and clean the fabric and turn them inside out to the side that wasn't faded and remake them. One of those coats was pure cashmere and a beautiful blue. My daughter got many a year out of that one. We even got our mitts on a whole seal skin coat in great shape, nothing can compare to the warmth of that. So my daughter was learning the importance of no money and we both could skirt around the issue and no one was the wiser.

When I got my share of money from Old Bess after she died. I spent it as fast as I could so the Missus didn't have a chance to get her claws on it. Now about the same time I supposedly won a train set for the boys but it needed an expensive transformer to run the outfit. I ran over and bought it right quick like no body's business. Next I headed out to trade in my '56 Chevy for a new sky blue Fairland 500 that I had been salivating over. I took my daughter to see a fine tooled leather purse my Missus had been crabbing about. It was behind lighted glass at Dayton's and looked like a piece of art, cost as much too. I moseyed my daughter over to the sweater department and bought her the finest mohair sweater that was in fashion. She could hardly believe it. It felt good to see her light up.

The feeling didn't last long and neither did the gift. After a few weeks Asked my daughter why she wasn't wearing the sweater. She gave me a stilted look and said that the Missus had told her I wanted it back. I did a little research and yep, the Missus had returned both items and pocketed the money. Damn I was mad

I gave up on gifts after that and became a bit cagier. If she was going to pull that kind of business she could pull it on someone else. But I never saw the worst coming down the pike.

I had a secret account with my daughter that I would match dollar for dollar. That was the way I helped her to learn to save money. It was just between her and me, or so I thought. By the time she graduated from high school she had over three thousand dollars in that account, which was enough for a car and first and last on an apartment in those days. We marched down to get the money after she graduated, and low and behold the Missus had finagled the money out of both our names, yep she had absconded with it. She stole from her own daughter's life-savings from baby sitting and waitressing all those years. A mother stealing from her daughter! I believe she would have stole the pennies off her mothers own corpse, probably did too. We both shook our heads in disgust at the bank; it took us a while to recover from that one. We sat in a diner downtown and could not even talk. there was no way I could make it up to my daughter.

That's not to say I let it slide. When the time came at work to resign my pension benefits I pondered awhile. Then I marched in the office and when my turn came I took a step I never looked back from. I took the Missus name off my pension. She would not get any pension when I died. I would only be worth while to her alive. I never looked back from that decision.

Chapter 14

Grub

Can you smell those beans? Oh my God, that is my weakness. Nobody makes beans like my daughter. Smell them! They've been simmering for over twelve hours. It's enough to drive me crazy. I don't want to move. Who's he? That's her husband. I think the smell of those beans is too much for him too. He comes by just to see how she is. We'll probably play a game of chess out back later, when you piss off.

There is nothing like enjoying a meal. I remember working with the C.C.C.'s in the Black Hills. We had simple fare but after a days work, we would all sit around the camp fire and enjoy the scenery and the companionship.

Beans. I ate beans everywhere I could, traveling in boxcars with the other bums. We got off the rails at the great Tetons and ate our pintos at sunset. Just like being in church it was, gazing at those peaks. What can you compare that to?

In the beginning, with the Missus we didn't have much. Like I told you before it was mainly cinnamon and hot rice for breakfast, topped with hot rice and milk for lunch and maybe spam and rice for dinner, if we were lucky. We had a few hunters in the family so bear and moose showed up right proper. I wasn't one for fish but there was an excess of it. Elk and deer blessed out table. I even caught two huge snapping turtles and wrestled them into a fifty gallon steel drum. I almost lost my arm doing it. They weren't stupid and managed to make a quick getaway in the night by tipping the drum over. I wish I could have seen that one.

With the better job the grub improved. My Missus did take over the kitchen after I nearly leveled it a few times smoking with the gas on. The menu never varied from week to week but we ate it just the same. You can always tell a meal made by loving hands and ours weren't.

I wanted my kids to be exposed to good food and manners. It is an education in itself and it can be an important show of respect to comport yourself properly around a good meal.

Every Sunday possible I hauled the herd out to the finest restaurant I could afford. This meant dresses and suits, civilized behavior to go with it. Not easy for the likes of us and a bit risky as well. We worked our way around the cutlery, the use of table linen and glass ware. Everyone learned menus and ordering in a timely manner, if necessary studying the menu beforehand. It weren't easy with our clan. It took great maneuvering but an empty stomach is a great motivator.

Appetizers were worked on, shrimp cocktail, fruit compote and marinades. Soon enough we worked on salads, tossed, quartered and graduated to waldorf and cobb. We delved into entrees and became acquainted with flame broil, filet mignon, porterhouse and rib eyes. Fish could be battered, broiled, marinated, barbequed or smoked.

The long list of vegetables sauntered by. Potatoes could be baked or baked twice, scalloped, augratin, mashed or new. Corn came steamed, on the cob and creamed. Spinach I generally liked creamed with bacon, I rarely had to share. Being in the Midwest the kids were firm believers in catsup on everything, it never appealed to me. Like they say, "you can take the mule out of the mountain but not the mountain out of the mule."

Desserts were easier to maneuver, apple pie, French apple, cherry compote and pumpkin pie. We enjoyed our share of chocolate pie, and rhubarb crumble. We even made it to baked Alaska and cherries jubilee.

Even with all plans made, some one would jump the track every once and awhile. Once the boys were using the toilet while we were waiting to be seated and taking all too much time. They finally emerged. The youngest was crying and the oldest had a nice set of urine lines across his knees. They knocked it off and we sandwiched the oldest between us, no one the wiser.

When food was not a good motivator for decent behavior, I did what I promised I would do. I went and parked the car directly in front of the restaurant's windows and waited for a seat in front of the car. I left the boys in the car to contemplate their actions and watch the rest of us enjoy our fine meal. I did what I promised and only had to do it twice as I recall.

As for myself, beans will always be my downfall, and comfort. Beans saw me though many a cold and lonely night. I will always have a warm spot in my heart for beans. I even crept down a hospital corridor before I had my kidney stones removed and polished off three plates. When I snuck back to my room, damn if that nurse wasn't waiting for me with that enema bag. Oh well. I tried. It was still worth it.

Funny what food can do. It was rhubarb strawberry pie that introduced me to real love.

Chapter 15

Relatively Speaking

Do you hear that song "Crazy"? I love that song, it could have been my theme song. It is such a shame Patsy Cline died so young. What feelings she put in her songs. It brings me back to the times out at the lake on the weekends. I'd sit nursing my root beer just listening to those sad songs. I'd talk low to the bar tender about my lost love. He'd quietly nod. I was so melancholy a time or two there. Funny how music can do that to you. That bar tender understood. Some times he'd sing sweet and low. I'd play the harmonica or just whistle my guts out.

What was I doing out there? I was marooned there while my Missus visited her relatives. How lucky for me. With her sixteen brothers and sisters and their hordes of kids visiting their parents it just wasn't my cup of tea. Of course, I didn't fit in. After ten minutes or so I'd get itchy, then cagey.

I could not understand the likes of them. It would be a perfectly fine day and all those big hulks would be crouched inside. They'd wile away the hours sipping on their beer like baby bottles and gossiping in Polish. Not my way to throw away a Saturday.

I will admit it was interesting place out in the sticks near Saint Cloud. The house was a two story sick green tar paper. It had no electricity, and a hand water pump in the kitchen. It looked at little more sturdy than the out buildings that looked ready to collapse if someone sneezed. There were three bedrooms, one downstairs for Grandma and Grandpa and two rooms upstairs, one for girls and one for boys. Out back, you could find the two holer. Yes I will admit I locked one of the brothers of the herd in there one snowy night. We had made our way out there in our jockeys through the snow. I, being in my pitiful stupor for lack of sleep, forgot he was along. After I was finished I just threw the bear lock on and proceeded to meander back to the bed and threw myself back on the pile of male bodies. No, he didn't freeze to death but he did have to beat his way out of there. He took it right hard too, like I had meant it. Anyway, out further back by the river was a trap door that was the opening to a cave of sorts. It was below the frost line and served as a so called natural refrigerator. This house had even been struck twice by lightening, does that tell you anything?

Grandma was an interesting case. She could throw one arm around you and hug you like you just came back from the dead, with the other arm she'd grab a shotgun and blast away at a raccoon out through the kitchen window. It could make your teeth itch. She always kept the kitchen table out in the yard except for meal times. Grandma was not stupid. She would have been cooking all day if the table would not have been outside. The boys hauled the table in at mealtimes and the herd came in and no one dawdled. If you missed, oh well.

The place was down right spotless. All the mattresses were hand made from goose down and the huge comforters on top were too. You crawled in and sunk in and prayed you'd keep breathing, but it was like sleeping on a cloud. No one, no exception went into Grandma and Grandpa's bedroom which was reported to have a thicker down mattress and comforter.

Now, put together sixteen beer drinking bored kids and their mates in one small room. Throw in a huge bunch of grand kids with no supervision out back, mix well and you guessed it. That's why I finally just dropped off my Missus and said my "How Dee Do." I threw away ten minutes or so, then hung out by the lake. Those big hulks would put the squeeze on me right quick if I stayed any longer. I married the runt; you would have thought they would be grateful. That wasn't enough. If I hung around, they would squeeze me out of a meal. They'd steal it right off my plate. Then they'd start squeezing me out of my place at the table. Slow, slow torture. I admit I was the odd man out, the uncivilized one. I learned and pissed off right quick.

I'd head out to the lake to whistle my guts out. I could contemplate my lost love and all around enjoy myself. Later in the afternoon, I'd head back to pick up the hoard of kids and get them the hell away from there for their own safety. We'd swim, fish, play ball or just act half daft, any thing before the drunken fighting would start. I always enjoyed being with the kids even if it was cold or snowing. I'd haul them behind the car with ropes to ski or sled, with all the rest of them packed eyeball to eyeball in the car like sardines to keep warm. We had a great time even if for a few hours. I did this because I do not trust drunks around kids. I don't trust drunks mainly anytime, that's a personal rule. I never trust them around kids. I never wanted them around my only daughter at all.

I managed to skirt around the fray of relatives but I do admit I messed up twice. One New Year's Eve we went over to the Missus sister's to celebrate. It was an adults only thing. It started innocent enough. They passed around appetizers with the beer and I was daft enough and hungry enough to lose my edge. Then over dinner which consisted of spaghetti, a food if you can call it that. It seems more like a communist plot to me. After this incident I swore off it completely. I was hungry and the food was brought out slow. I ate it anyway and saw no water or milk to wash it down with, I stooped to wine. Dessert was some kind of rum cake served with mixed drinks at midnight.

As you can imagine it took me about three hours to drive five miles home. I had to carry the Missus up the outside stairs, as she was passed out cold. Good thing too, as I forgot my keys in the ignition and had to deposit her carcass on the top of the stairs. She promptly rolled off the top and down the drive. I just dragged her back to the stairs and I managed to get the key in the lock after another hour or so. I froze my behind off on those stairs. I thought I saw those blond headed kids of mine watching the whole production from the windows. I couldn't blame them a bit. I rightly would have paid them to open the door, but at that point I was past all speech.

I did stir later the next day from my bed, the fact was I could not breathe. The doctor patched me up stating I had busted my ribs. So there you go, I had stooped to vomiting over the fence as the custom was, that way you didn't mess up the hosts yard. I didn't even remember doing it. Lucky me.

After that, something miraculous happened. If her relatives came over and I got pinned up against the wall and the table during dinner as was the custom, the best thing happened. I got allergic. Yep, I would wind up and start sneezing right proper. Once I got as high as eighty one sneezes in a row. Even with both hands over my mouth it was quite indecent and disturbing, especially given the fact I started sneezing a fair while into the meal. Once I commenced sneezing, I could rightly clear them clean out of the house. I could do it in record time, even for Pollacks. It cured me from being around the relatives. It was my secret weapon, but really it was a God send.

Chapter 16

Old Spice

Hey, look at that. Bold as brass. See, that car over there, the One with the born again Christian fish sign on the back. I bet God is real proud of that eight ball. First off that car rightly needs a baptism. How can you advertise you are a believer in God and drive around in a filthy clunk like that? Never ceases to amaze me.

I tried to learn from my nasty wayward past. Prison taught me to love cleanliness. In prison you had a three minute shower break three times a week. It was shear heaven, even without the Old Spice or Aqua Velva. Funny thing what a little soap and water can do for your attitude. If you're tired, cold water can rightly liven you up. If your wound up, a hot bath can bless you with a baby's sleep. Not all people hold this view. By me, it is a true luxury to keep clean.

It always amazes me people who say they are so religious. Why don't they put there money where their mouth is, clean their own bodies, homes and spread it out from there. Isn't that God's plan, shouldn't we be taking care of our inheritance as mortals? More importantly, the mind is a good place to start. Do people think that God is deaf, dumb and blind, or only hope he is? Get off your knees and clean something and your attitude will follow.

Now, as far as my family was concerned I was in charge of my outfit, that only left me to run it like prison. That was all I knew. Having three children there's the rub; right off you're out numbered. All in all, it usually ran pretty smooth. I handled the laundry. Everyone was responsible for their area. Most personal things were kept under your bed just like the big house. My daughter handled the dusting, Saturday and Sunday she ploughed her way through the ironing.

Washing dishes proved to be a big bone of contention. From an early age with a step stool there stood my daughter washing and drying the dishes. The sad part for me what that it could have been a friendly time spent with her mother building a relationship, or at the least a time of peace and quiet. My Missus turned up the drama most every night just as she was finishing, then inspections started. Next thing you know, all the dishes came down and then some. Next thing she'd be bullied into wiping down all the insides of the cupboards. On and on it went. After three hours or so, she would stumble off to bed with no time for home work. She would rise with me a quarter to five and start in on that. Not much of a life. Dang if I knew what to do about it.

Damn if I knew what the Missus did all day. That's the sixty four thousand dollar question. When I came home from work she was still in her pajamas, quite a deterrent for most of my kid's friends. She had an intimate relationship with the telephone. Then again to throw us off the track, she would vacuum for hours after midnight.

I even found out she left the kids locked in the house alone. One of my police buddies informed me of an inquiry he made at my residence. My neighbors heard my daughter screaming for help and called the police. They found out she had been left alone with the boys and locked in without a phone. She was bathing the boys when the youngest started chocking on a hard candy. I can imagine she had been trying everything. The Missus arrived right before the coppers and cleaned up the vomit and mess. I'm sure she threatened the kids; my buddy said my daughter was too scared to speak. The coppers weren't stupid and gave the Missus quite a little pep talk on mother hood with a vivid description of her duties behind bars. That kept her act under ground for quite a while. That, and the fact I asked them to take a buzz down the neighborhood now and again for the hell of it. She became right paranoid and thought she was under siege.

About the same time my oldest boy cured the dish torture. I wished I could have thought up that scheme. My Missus got the brilliant idea it was now time for my boy to help with the drying of the dishes. She thought she would have them both planted there for hours. My boy had other plans. First thing you know he smiles at his sister beside him, and takes one of those depression plates and slings it square to the floor. All hell broke loose. We cleaned up the mess and he was so sorry. What an innocent look he could throw on. I tell you, what a brilliant move. It was a repeat performance with a couple of glasses thrown in the following night. The kids were told to go to their rooms, exactly where they wanted to be in the first place. Here this six year old solved this torture for all of us in two days. The maneuvers I learned from my son that day came in right handy later on. My missus would not let any of us near the kitchen after that. How sad.

Chapter 17

Off My Rocker

Enough said about cleanliness, we all know it is next to godliness. It really doesn't mean a thing if you are not organized. In the big house organization was easy. You had a cell, everything was at a minimum, not a bad thing really. Riding the rail or under a tent helps you get the idea down.

The problem for me was family life, I was responsible for five. It was real shit soup. To top it off the Missus was a collector of rubber bands, glass bottles, tin cans. Most of the time I did the best I could and left it at that. A house is kind of like a living thing really, if it is always taking things in, it can get down right constipated. A main stickler with me was the garage, of course the Missus knew it made me edgy and put the spurs to it. She loved making the garage a bone of contention. Once my little one fixed that problem and at about three years of age decided to take a drive for himself and drove clean though the back of the garage. Not much damage was done to the structure because of the collection of cans and toilet paper buffeting the onslaught.

This one time in particular I knew she was winding up. Similar to the time she insisted on changing the storm windows right when I had the kid's packed up to go on the Easter egg hunt. I got the bright idea from my boy's dish washing and just ran though the house and threw out the windows before she could catch them. I got back in the car in no time flat with the kid's and off we went. Now it was a different story.

She knew there was a big wrestling match going on that Saturday afternoon and had been starting in on me about the garage. Not to worry. I had it all planed out. I got the day off work. When her royal highness was sleeping I took the kids out for a big breakfast for a pre attack feast. We could get through most of the day on that grub. We crept back at about seven in the morning and I got busy. I parked the car on the street. I took a radio out to the garage along with a loaf of bread and peanut butter. I already had my thermos filled with coffee at the restaurant, just in case I got running on empty half way through. I got busy and masked the windows with newspapers. I shut and locked it up from the inside. My boy was to get ready to haul out the old lumber from the back window. She was too lazy to go behind the garage. We would burn it later in the day. It was a brilliant plan.

I turned on that radio and started in. I danced around and threw everything in fifty gallon steel drums I had already stashed in there. Yep, I busted every damn jar and bottle in sight. Most of it had no business being in there in the first place. An example being a couple thousand rolls of emergency toilet paper. I "accidentally" got those wet. I flattened every type of tin can known to man, like it there was a third world war we'd need ten thousand cans per person. Go figure.

Oh yah, she went banging on that door a few times with her pajamas on. She backed off when the neighbors started peeking out. She sent the kids out a few times but they were already working on my side. They played it well though and looked quite edgy just for added suspense. I just cranked up the radio and started by whistling real shrill like.

In all that mess I finally found all my tools and arranged them. I found out I had as many as eight sets of some wrenches. What a waste. My oldest boy grabbed the lumber and the combustibles out of the back window. Then he passed me a hose and I cleaned and scrubbed it all out and opened the garage door. There I stood and the dust settled around me.

The Missus headed out to survey the damage. She did a real simper dance. She avoided me like the plague and headed in the house to call the relatives and report that I had gone off my rocker again. Perfect. That gave me the time to start the fire in the back yard and hose down the driveway. Hell, I even had some time left over so I cleaned and vacuumed out the Ford Fairlane.

I mossied in the house and polished off my victory with crackers and milk for supper. I wasn't stupid, she wouldn't be cooking dinner for me, that was a given. I sauntered into the living room and sat myself in the red rocker ready for wrestling. My kids joined me on the couch. I was feeling right fine, so carried away with my accomplishments.

Wrestling got red hot, it was a real drama. Verne the champion was almost getting killed again. Well. I started getting up and throwing in my personal commentary. Then I'd back myself in my rocker. It went like this for quite a spell. Every time I'd plant my butt back in that chair it was further away from the T.V., but I wasn't paying proper attention. I was all worked up and lurching all over the place. No I didn't put my fist through that television, not that time anyway. But as it turned out the cord was wrapped around the rocker. I don't care if you don't believe me.

That was the least of my worries anyway as I lost it completely and rocked clear backwards out of that living room window. Holy hell what a mess. There was glass and drapes and shredded window shades all around me, right on that drive way I had just cleaned. I landed like a long tailed black cat still sitting upright in that damn red rocker. I was quite stunned for a second or two, but my kids just kept on laughing.

After that I was quite famous around the neighborhood and my kids even started wanting to sell seating tickets to be able to come over and watch me, while I watched television. Damn kids.

Chapter 18

Cold Comfort

Yea, I know pain. It comes in many forms. Pain can sneak up on you slowly and wrap you in a blanket of illness. Once in awhile, you open the door and there it is bold as brass and your foots smashed. I lost my mother early on and never got over that slow ache. When, I was rejected by my father, for our differences, that was a different bitter bite.

At seventeen I was working out my time on a Montana ranch. I was so cold and abandoned. I never felt the horses drive the cart over my foot in that blizzard. It didn't make much difference either way. I had to try and save the farmer's little girl. I had to get her home from school. I could only lead the horses by feeling along the top of the fence posts. I was completely blind in that white out. I couldn't feel my foot anyway. I was frozen.

Later, when I got my foot repaired, it hurt like hell, but it was a good pain. I had to ability to have it repaired. I had choice. It threw a monkey wrench in my Missus routine. It did her a bit of good to have her cage rattled. When that damn priest came over with that slimy bastard attorney, he actually proceeded to threaten the Missus at my kitchen table. She had not been making her pledge, which was my proper money. I listened to that bastard threaten my Missus in those low tones. You know how I am. My head began to burn. I lurched up out of that bedroom and had that crutch up against his hammy neck in no time flat.

Thank Christ I had the capacity to teach my kids about all kinds of pain. One minute I could be picking teeth out of one boy's head after hockey, then the next I had to teach my daughter how to pinch a leg so she could endure me yanking off her blood blisters from the money rings. I'd just turn and a knee would be presented to me after an altercation on a skate board.

That's when my feminine side kicked in. Go ahead and laugh. I don't mind. I comforted the children the best I could. I patched them up and usually could tell them how stupid they had been.

Remember the time my daughter got that head full of tackle? I had to do some mighty fast thinking that time. I was out in the sticks. I bought a bit of rum and mixed it with some wild blueberries and milk. It proved to be a bad combination stain wise. It did put her to sleep. I pushed those barbs all the way further in. Then, I got a hold of the barbs and cut 'em off and pulled 'em through. I even saved most of her hair. That was the closest I came to brain surgery.

Go ahead and criticize me. You can even call me a sissy. I always talk about the kids as mine. Maybe I didn't birth them but I was their mother just the same. They were my kids at the end of the day and my full responsibility. I always told them their mother was their mother in the same sense that a cow or a pig is a mother, that's all. Either way I didn't have time to think about it. I was too busy trying to do it.

What did throw me off the tracks was illness. I'm not a firm believer in it. It's different with kids. They'd come home all covered in spots and miserable. Whoa. Everything comes to a halt.

I was real lucky one year. My kids managed to get the measles and mumps at the same time. The Missus would not allow any thing sick upstairs. So screw it. I took the mattress and made a make shift hospital right in the basement. I called off work. The first couple of days I was in heaven. I just slept with them non stop. That way I could change the sheets and hose them down whenever necessary.

I just lay there during those starry nights and look up out that basement window. I had my kids piled around me. I could smell their damp necks and feel their fine downy hair. Their small hands and feet snaking out to touch me. How lucky could a guy like me get? I was with my kids and it was peaceful. I took a drag on my cigarette and was grateful to the big man up there. I could have ridden "Old Sparky." I never thought I would get this far.

Chapter 19

Cowboy Love

This evening you can smell roses. There they are over there, proud and chest high. I have always had a weakness for roses. Each type is so different, has its own personality and ways. If I close my eyes and think back, I only remember my one true love with that smell.

I had just gotten sprung from the slammer and returned home to see good old Dad. Not the best idea. I missed my two sisters and had a confab or two with them. I was just walking slow and enjoying the evening coming on. The birds were scrambling to nest. Roses were in the air, thick and heavy. That's when my nose pricked up to another scent. There is a scent that drives me wild and brings me to my knees, the aroma of which I could fight and die for. My head was in a spin.

Yep. Pie. I stopped dead in my tracks. My nose did a quick survey and led me smack dab to a small home with a window ledge. The curtains were fluttering. There on that ledge, it was sitting to cool. My nose did a quick survey. Rhubarb it was, packed in strawberries. There was even a hint of cinnamon and it had a crumble top. Could my life get better? The only problem between me and that pie were strategically placed rose bushes under the sill. I had to admit, that was a smart cook but no great shakes for the life of me.

I crept up real quiet like. I let my jean clad behind push those thorns away from my destination. I slipped right under that sill and wedged myself in. I closed my eyes. I let my nose waltz around a sweet time. Nostrils quivering. I don't rightly know how much time passed. If somebody had hit me in the head with a shovel, it would have been a happy death. Something better happened, my eyes opened to the most beautiful apparition. My jaw went slack and I couldn't blink.

There she was those clear blue eyes looking clean back. There was a mass of fuzzy chestnut hair and the most beautiful smile. She was just a petite thing, not your normal sized Mid-West cook.

"Sir, you wouldn't be sizing up my pie to steal?"

"I hate to admit to contemplating that very thing Miss."

"Then Sir, may I invite you to take a seat on the front porch and I'll directly bring you out a slice. That way there will be no further temptation."

That's how my cowboy love started. I wrenched my scrawny behind from those roses. I sat on that porch as if in the palace of the Queen of England. This might never happen again. Soon a thick slice of warm pie draped with thick cream parked itself right in front of me, with a steaming cup of coffee. I took my time with that pie, like I was on a world tour. I stretched it out as long as possible.

She sat on the porch swing and fanned herself in the warm autumn air. Her dress fluttered as she swung slowly. I was hypnotized like a Florida gator. The evening air was scented with roses, warm pie and the smell of a clean fresh woman. Her perfume meandered over, was it Blue Waltz?

Did she know she was in the presence of a criminal, a killer, a jail bird? I stalled as long as possible; I didn't want it to come to an end.

"You must be Margaret's brother. She's been waiting so long to see you. We quilt together on Tuesdays at the church. She is so happy to have you back."

Then she smiled and got up. She went into the house and brought out another slice and refilled my cup. She knew. It didn't bother her. I don't know what happened to me. I opened my mouth and told her things I had never told anyone. Nothing about me seemed to bother her in the least. She just looked straight at me and listened, like she had all the time in the universe. I kept myself in check and after about an hour I shut my mouth. I raised myself up and tipped my head and bid her a fair evening. I wrenched myself off that porch. Lord, I never thought love would happen. Not to me. If this was all there ever was, it would be just fine.

It didn't end there. I saddled up to many a fine desert on that porch, many a fine meal too. There was pleasant conversation. The type were someone talks and the other listens. We managed to find our way to a few picnic sites with her small daughter in tow. Her daughter was a lovely thing, looked just like her mama. She had come out wrong and had a gimpy leg. I always kept a close eye on her. I didn't want anything to happen to her, she looked so fragile.

So now you know and yes, this was a star crossed love. Yes, she was married and he was a rail road man. He was thirty odd years older. Her father more or less had sold her off to the Mormon geezer. It happened back then.

We tried to approach him on the subject. It wasn't like Carey was his only wife. She didn't matter to him. He was rarely around. When he made his fateful offer, we both knew. We stood there dumbfounded. Tears welled up in her eyes and her whole being slumped.

Now I am a bastard in many ways. I still could not stoop to separate a mother from her child. That was what that cruel bastard wanted. He didn't want the child. He'd just pack her off to one of his other wives to mistreat. I could not ask Carey to pay that price for the likes of me. I would not want her to. We both knew we could never live with ourselves if we did.

So there you have it. I left on the next boxcar headed to no where.

Chapter 20

Steam

After I lost my love, I did what a lot of people do, I traveled. I changed the scenery and joined the bums on the rails. I ate under the stars. We made stews with every can of something we could throw in. Every night in my dreams, I journeyed back to the arms of Carey. I touched her fuzzy hair, I smelled her sweet neck. I swung her daughter in my arms, and then I'd eat pie on the porch. I traveled. I traveled physically every day and each night I traveled mentally under the stars. I tried to work off some steam. I heard the other bum's sad stories. I held those moments, I wrapped them around me.

That's how I wound up in the Twin Cities, Saint Paul to be exact. I got a job as a security guard and met many a fine and wealthy person. I still a time or two went melancholy, but I kept my mind tired by keeping the body tired. Like the boxers say; kill the body and the mind dies. So that's how I walked off my steam as I call it. You can call it any thing you want, grief, anger, sadness, frustration or rage. It's all the same to me.

That's how I met Mr. Chang. Late one evening, I was walking off my steam with my steel tip boots. They came in mighty handy that night. I heard an odd damaged whimpering coming from an alley downtown. It was the back end of the Chinese Restaurant. I turned to face the whimpering and barely made out the crumpled Mr. Chang kneeling in the alley with his hands up to protect his face. There was a huge brute hovering over him. Now why in the hell would someone want to pick on that poor chink I didn't know? I figured it had to be a shake down for money. I heard a right unpleasant sound and identified it as brass knuckles. Mr. Chang fell over onto his side.

That is when I started down that alley like a half starved black cat. I felt my body going all springy like a rattle snake. I picked up a bottle quietly. There was no turning back, I blew. I let out years of steam on that bastard. I hit that thick skull with the bottle. I only used it once; stunned he dropped to his knees. That's when the steel toed boots come in right handy. I placed some nice damage to his kidneys and ribs. It didn't sound pleasant. He landed face down in alley water. I glanced at Mr. Chang and he still was lying on his side and breathing quite rough. I stooped over the thug and pulled off those brass knuckles, he was out cold, maybe dead.

I went over to Mr. Chang and picked him up and hauled him back into the back door of the restaurant. I deposited him in one of his tomato red plastic booths and headed back. I dragged that brute by the feet into the walk-in storage area of the restaurant and locked him in. I took a survey of the alley and nothing had stirred. I went back to Mr. Chang and noticed two chaps had appeared at his side, probably his sons. They were stoic but tears were running down their faces. Hell, they were running down my face too, but we didn't have time for it. We put our backs to it. They motioned for me to the stairs and I pulled Mr. Chang up and over my shoulder and parted the beaded curtains and headed up. That's when I met with what must have been Mr. Chang's wife and daughter huddled together.

I laid him down on one of those floor mattresses and tore open his shirt. It looked like he had some busted ribs but nothing was poking through. He face was a proper mess and one eye was completely closed. His skull was intact and I couldn't find any busted bones. The women took over and started patching him up. I headed back down the stairs, to survey the damage in the alley. Just in that moment of time those two young lads had cleaned up the mess and everything was tomb quiet. I then looked myself over, not a scratch or a drop of blood. I tried making it out the door but one of the young chaps led me out a side door. He tried talking to me but I just grabbed him by the shoulder and put one finger to my lips for silence.

I crept out of there and back to the boarding house. I slept like a baby. I let out years of steam that night. Funny thing, it felt good. Even the jokers at work commented on how rested I looked. I still figured anytime I'd be fingered by he police. I read the papers and listened to the radio. But I never heard any news. No news is good news.

I ran into Mr. Chang about five years later when I was parking cars at night at the Ballard Ramp. Mr. Chang came in to park his car. I didn't recognize him at first but he recognized me. He looked like a million dollars in a cut tailored suit and silk shirt. He drove a Cadillac. I introduced him to my little girl who was sitting in the office coloring and dressed her pajamas. He invited me to his restaurant any time.

Two days later, gifts arrived for me at work, Fanny Farmer Chocolates for me, my weakness. There was a vase of fresh cut flowers for the Missus and a red box for my daughter. In it were the most beautiful pink silk pajamas with embroidery just like those Chinese wear. I even took a photograph of her in them. See, there she is.

It didn't stop there. Damndest thing too. Once my daughter got in high school, she got a job at one of the hotels across from where I worked. She would wait for me to get off work and we would ride home together. For my birthday one year she arranged a dinner for us two after work. Guess where? Yep, at the Chinese Restaurant. Now I never ate Chinese before. I was always a might suspicious about eating a cat or a dog, let alone a dead body. I had to do it, but I did it under protest. She had arranged everything and I couldn't let her down.

There was Mr. Chang treating me like royalty. My daughter didn't quite understand all the attention I was getting. It was down right embarrassing, but good. So there we sat in that same tomato red plastic booth I had deposited Mr. Chang in over a decade prior. He brought out the biggest steak I had encountered in quite a while with a huge serving of mashed potatoes and fresh peas. I took my time and waltzed around that plate a good while. He served us himself and bowed while he was going it. Made me a bit cagey, but I survived. I even tested my daughter's dish, and decided I would make Chinese food more of a habit. I had a right fine conversation with my daughter. Just when I thought it was over, the lights dimmed. Out came those two sons all grown up with a cake with real fourth of July sparklers. It was my favorite, too, German chocolate. It was like the whole United Nations was singing happy birthday. I decided to go for broke and washed it down with some Jasmine tea in those tiny cups. My daughter pulled out two books I had been salivating over as my gift from her. How could she ever know what she had already done?

We finally took our leave and thanked everyone. We sauntered over to the parking lot to pick up the car nice and slow. We just enjoyed the evening and our bellies were happy too. I felt in my jacket pocket for my keys and my hand felt more than keys. In one pocket with the keys was another metal object, the brass knuckles. In the other pocket was a velvet pouch full of Chinese gold coins with a hand printed Chinese fortune that read, "For emergency only."

Chapter 21

Boomerang

No, I'm not one to put stock in the modern campfire called television. Communist plot as far as I'm concerned. Let's just drop our drawers and show the universe how damn dumb we really are. "Thank you God for the life, but I'd rather sit in front of this box until I rot. Then I'll have a pack of kids and hook up some real expensive crap to the box. My kids will acquire square eyeball syndrome. But at least I don't have to waste any time on my kids. It's not my problem they have brain rot. It must have been the teacher's fault. It can't be me. I didn't do anything. It ain't my fault my kid shot up twelve kids at school. I think I'll sue the government." No that's not my style.

I have to admit we did own a black box and we did a ritual of Sunday morning cartoons followed by wrestling. I could not help that I love to laugh. Anyway, I'd be sleeping on the living room floor, all stretched out. I'd slowly awake from my stupor and peek at my kids watching cartoons real quiet like. I'd keep up my snoring and enhance it quite a bit till they knew I was awake and they'd tackle me. Or if they were ignoring me I'd keep up my snoring and inch my way to one of their feet and bite it. I loved catching them off guard and they'd all pile on me. All hell would break loose.

My downfall was that damn wrestling. I was a sad addict. I still do like it. I know it's all Hollywood but I was always a goner. It was that damn Verne getting his ass kicked in by some bully. Like I didn't know that feeling? My bully was sleeping in a bed I bought and paid for. Oh, it could make my blood boil to see his title and belt being given to a real hard case.

All my kids knew the scissor hold, full Nelson, half Nelson and the dreaded pile driver. So this is how I educated my kids, go and say it. I can take it. Just remember they needed self defense, both physical and mental.

This is where I drew the line. School is important. I didn't want mental midgets. They were enrolled in private Catholic school, and I had to sell my soul to the Devil, so to speak. It became my job to teach the nuns to drive. That was so my Missus could get a discount on the education part. How much worse could my life get. So for the next blessed thirteen years I carted nuns around. I saw one car after another get dinged up. More than once I had to leap for my life and bail out. I just got to be too scared to hang on to the dash board any longer. To hell with the car, it usually made it home somehow. More than once I just hid in the bushes as the kid's school and waited to cool down so I could walk my kids home. One time walking home we all watched as my car's tires went down the hill without my car. I just had to stop and light a cigarette and scratch my head.

I guess the baby Jesus on the dash board did the best he could under the circumstances. Maybe I'd be better off with one of those glow in the dark Virgin Mary statues. At least I'd be fighting fire with fire. Hell, I'd even stoop to one of those rosaries blessed by the Pope if it could save my sky blue '56 Chevy. Oh well.

Most all of this education boomeranged on the Missus. The nuns took her aside more than once and started her in on a proper education in child rearing. They weren't stupid or blind. They noticed the missing hair, black eyes and bruises. My Missus actually started getting up and giving the kid's their medicines when they needed it.

They even gave her an education on the subject called breakfast. My daughter had been fainting in the church waiting for communion. You know, the body of Christ. My wife loved sending them off early before school to go to mass. The nuns took her aside and in more words than one impressed upon my Missus the need for grub. Not that the Missus did get her behind up to make anything but cereal boxes were put out regular and the lock came off the fridge. They were allergic to most cereal and sneezed a good deal of it around the place but what the hell, it was an improvement.

Another thing that stuck in the craw of the nuns was the fact the Missus would not allow the use of the word mother, mom, or maw. No siree. That was not good enough, she wanted a title. Like the Queen of England she wanted to be called Madam. My kids were great at distortion and Madam got to be drawn out quite to distraction. Maaaaw Daaaam. You can imagine. They weren't stupid. Neither were the nuns and the Missus got put in her place once again.

Yep, my kids got their education. My cars got dings and destroyed. The Missus got her private lessons on staying between the lines, the nuns kept her in check.

Chapter 22

Wings

Now I do believe in honesty as the best policy. I never hid anything about myself, especially to my kids. Yet, I am a firm believer that it should be on a need to know basis. My kids knew I had made some poor choices. They knew our house was not a home. I didn't have to explain that.

Like I said before, I regularly lined them up. I'd pace back and forth and put on quite a show. I'd rant about all the things wrong with me and how I was a bastard in many ways. Then I'd point my finger at them and mention the difference between them and me. That being their mother's blood. They didn't see it as a joke at first but they soon caught on.

There are definite lines you should not cross with your kids. My Missus was preening my oldest son to take my place. If anything would happen to me, like an accident? He could step up to the plate. I knew something was fishy. Once in awhile, we took a family vote, like the time on freedom from religion. He just happened to hesitate and look up at the Missus. That's all I needed to know. He was courting favors from the Missus and had to perform like a trained monkey. Just like the mob, it was an offer you could not refuse. Soon your on your knees and can't get out. Married to the mob or married to the Missus what is the difference? There are sons who can't break from their mothers. Scary. Very twisted. Good serial killer material. The only thing you hope is that you never find them in bed together, as far as I knew this never happened.

As far as my business is concerned, I kept it on the hush. If I needed help in the sexual department, I went to a professional. I didn't need any more problems in my life with a stupid affair. I didn't want more drama with the Missus or my kids dragged through any mud. I never needed to degrade my Missus; she managed that all by herself.

One of my Missus more glowing moments happened when my daughter was in the hospital. She was born with a deformed spine. You would have never known it; she was always hanging upside down from the willow or cart wheeling around the yard. By then, she was out of the house and married. I wasn't impressed with the smell of her husband, but he had to be a cake walk compared to life with the Missus. I recall she must have been about twenty years old.

We went to the hospital to pay a visit, in separate cars, of course. I thought I had beaten the Missus to the room. I helped my daughter to take her first steps after surgery. I even bought her a pink robe. We started out innocently enough and she was doing right fine. We slowly made our way down past the sun room. For some reason, we both glanced in.

Bam, there the Missus was. She was curled up like a spider on a hot stove right in the lap of my daughter's flea bag of a husband. We just wavered like deer in the headlights. They had their backs to us and she was running her fingers of one hand though his hair. You don't want to know what she was doing with the other.

There we stood on the gates of purgatory. That was a nice slice of honesty in front of us which we could have done without. We finally found our feet and kept shuffling past the door. My daughter made it a little farther and slumped her head against the wall. Tears fell on that new pink robe. God in heaven, please! What can you do for a daughter who has suffered such indignity and theft by her mother's own hand?

I choked out whispered words and led my daughter back to the room. We got our composure back just in time. Those two snakes put in their appearances and finally slithered out. My daughter and I had a tight confab that day. It was an honest heart to heart. In the finish, she made the promise not to stay with him. There was no reason. It was a different day and age. Otherwise, I would have planned a one way fishing trip for that young buck but she had given me her word.

It took her only ten years to get out. She planned it better than Eisenhower. She had the patience from standing in front of the ironing board. She used the education from the school of hard knocks. I offered to help her in any way I could along the way. She didn't need it. She was a woman, full and grown. She had her wings and flew from the nest. I couldn't be happier. She had self reliance. Isn't that what parenting is all about?

Chapter 23

Deef

Yea, you don't have to remind me, I know I'm deef. Best thing that ever happened to me too. I always looked forward to the day I could not hear the Missus. It just kind of did creep up on me though. But I can still listen.

I listened to many things in my day. The feet of my cockroach in solitary bringing me a note from a buddy. I always loved God's symphony of the crickets under a starry night. I loved to hear the pages of a favorite book in my hand. There are two sounds I highly prize. Water. Listening to it slapping on the sides of a floating rowboat. The insulating silence of snow flakes falling. Shower drops giving your body back energy. Ice cracking beneath your feet, reminding you that your very small indeed. The other sound was that of my kid's laughter, a highly prized commodity. I loved the giggles with their arms around my neck. Snorts after someone did something daft, usually me. The silent and contained smiles for very serious places.

Many people never have to listen and others just refuse. There are some with their yaps open telling you what you ought to be doing. Others are so arrogant they even want to tell God what he should be doing. Can you believe that? If they only shut their yaps and really listened, they could actually hear what God is trying to tell them.

Listening clued me in on the Missus mood. It kept me vigilant and heading problems off at the pass. Listening to my kids kept bad idea's from germinating.

I was always a sucker for music. It always belched out of our house and I have a whistle so shrill it can peel your eyelids off. We always had a reason to listen, to sing and to dance, good or bad we danced. I remember back and we did the required polka. The kids learned all kinds of folk dances. I was told I was very poor at waltzing, but I got out and shoved myself around anyway. You have to take into account my bum back and floppy foot. If my Missus seemed to mind, my kids never did. We'd hook up the record player in the garage and soon a pack of kids from the neighborhood would be in there on a rainy afternoon. I even remember my youngest with his regulation saddle shoes learning the twist when he was about three. I couldn't believe he could do it. There he was tow hair and freckles with my daughter's encouragement.

I will admit, I am no prize to listen to. Popeye has nothing on me. My voice is as gravely as quarry stone. I put the clampers on opening my mouth, as much as possible anyway. I had less problems with the Missus that way. Once in awhile my mouth would open up and I couldn't trust myself with what would come out.

That is exactly what happened one day out shopping. I left my girl in the shoe department to get some school shoes. When I snuck back, there he was. A shoe salesman with a huge finger pointed down at my daughter. He was berating my kid. I listened to that bag of wind tell my ten year old daughter that she should be accompanied by her mother when buying shoes. That it was improper, blah, blah, blah. My daughter couldn't help it. She had been hauling herself and her brothers around since she was five. She was perfectly capable. She even took them to the doctor and dentist on the bus. I listened to this liver lipped shoe sales man, I looked at my poor freckled faced daughter just taking it.

Bam, my veins popped in my head and my scalp prickled, I swooped down right behind him like Dracula. Sure I was a foot shorter and maybe lighter by a hundred pounds but he was no match for the likes of me. My daughter took one look and smiled and moved back out of the line of fire. I opened my mouth and let out some of that gravel pit. I told him he had better close his mouth and do his job and keep his opinions to himself. Not quite in those terms. I had quite an audience forming at that point. I added with a bit of verbal flourish that in the future he should try to stick to picking on some one his own size, or at least my size.

Once I got started it took me a while to crank myself down. I noticed the store manager peering down from his second floor glass window. Then, over the intercom, that liver lipped sales man was called into that office and a nice woman came over to finish waiting on us. My daughter tried those shoes on standing up. She was too proud to sit down and try them on. She had had enough. We exited hand in hand and I glanced up to the manager's office and there was liver lips getting a big fat finger pointed at him. Oh well. He finally had his big yap shut.

We both needed to cool down a bit, and we sauntered off to Walgreen's Drug and had a vanilla malt. We sat there a fair while and I eyeballed my daughter and we both just cracked up laughing. I patted that shoe box like an Olympic Medal.

We sat on the back yard swing many an evening and relived old liver lips. It's true my daughter never talked much. But those wheels were turning just the same. She was one of those kids that learn from others mistakes. Any one who has a kid like that is truly blessed.

Okay I'll tell you one more for the road. My daughter and I went to get an ice cream at the Dairy Queen. We got up to the window to order and we heard this imbecile order a pint of ice cream from his car. Nothing spectacular about that, except he pronounced it phonically as in rhyming with hint. I looked down at my kid and commented that it sounded like my oldest boy's best friend. I would even wager a bet with her. Yep, we peeked around the corner of the building and we were dead right. Once again we just cracked up laughing.

Chapter 24

Snake Eyes

You back for more are you? Fine, come sit a spell with me on the patio, that way we won't disturb my daughter. I just want to have a smoke. I enjoy being out here on a fine night. It makes me glad to see my daughter and to see the investment I made in my kids paid off . Kids are a crapshoot. You roll the dice; you never know for sure how it will all come about. I am no different from anyone. I wanted much better for my kids. I did what I could so they would have it better. Not with money, time was my investment. I gave them as much of myself as I could.

Then slowly the kids started emerging from the dragon's lair. Which path would they follow? Would it be a dark one?

Physically these kids were strong. Nine times out of ten, you could not find them at the house. The neighborhood was rank with children. Most everyone knew about our house and only a brave few dare enter. However, on our property behind the garage was a marvel of nature, a sublime ancient weeping willow. That tree, despite the atmosphere of our house, became ground zero of all the comings and goings of the neighborhood kids.

Superstition flew over the back yard, many were the suppositions that this tree been planted on ancient Indian burial ground, or deadly quick sand. Many a night I thought it might be cursed by a love that had died in the swamp where the willow stood upright and proud. Mix the neighborhood lore and the popular tales of Tarzan and you guessed it. That tree was the meeting place of every pint-sized kind in a four-block radius.

That willow supported the shenanigans of all those kids or just one. Never did I see anyone really get hurt in it either. On weekends, it resounded like a huge subtropical mango with brightly colored parrots-kids squawking and flying between the ground touching limbs. This tree held all the secrets, ours and many generations before us. It had seen many a thing or two. In the heat of the summer we would take our raggedy blankets up there and a makeshift tent would emerge.

Once, our back neighbor invested in a new fangled swing set for her back yard. I think the kids took this as a personal challenge. They took right off to perch and swing all over it. Proudly the neighbor crossed her arms and proclaimed her investment would lure the children in her back yard. The children perked up their ears and looked back at the willow.

Nothing could quite compete for the love of that tree. It took less than thirty minutes for those kids to coordinate their movements. In that amount of time, that new fancy dancy swing set had its baptism by fire and the result was twisted uprooted wreckage. They ran back to the open arms of the willow and no further investments were made.

The willow cradled, listened and held not only my kids but did so for any forlorn young passer by. That tree swaddled and held them in camouflaged peace. No kid could be found in that tree except by choice. Any kid's paradise was up there, toy army men lined some branches, Barbie dolls others. Many a chess and checker game played out above ground. Any number of books, blankets and pillows were scattered up there. Only once, did it take out the neighborhood electricity when all the kids decided on a Tarzan marathon and the power lines were wrenched from the adjacent pole.

In storms those branches kept you dry, and the winds rocked you to sleep. Despite its height lightening never hit it. A time or two when we felt our hair stand on end during an electrical storm we came from the house and threw ourselves under the mercy of the willow. Its protection was unwavering.

Many a dark night I saw my daughter make her way silently across the lawn to the willow. She made her way from her basement cell with her blanket in tow. She left behind the vacuuming, nagging and banging doors. She fled like a refugee to the arms of that willow. I envied her falling asleep under a curtain of night's stars. Once or twice I snuck out to have a cigarette and look at her perched up there with her Raggedy Ann doll. She slept quietly. I held hope that her dreams would take her far, far away to a peaceful space. I did not have to worry, the willow held her secure swaying with the breeze. It quietly rocked my child to sleep like a mothers secure arms.

Funny thing, it was like that tree understood. That willow had a huge capacity for compassion. When the children grew and left, the heart of the willow disappeared. That powerhouse of security died. It had served its purpose.

Chapter 25

For Louie

Now I want to talk about self regulation here. You can call it what you like, self discipline, self control. When you boil it right down, it is important. Its reward is self respect. It's basic. If a person can't learn early on, it gets much harder in life. One can learn easy from your parent's example or you can learn it hard. Like so many examples of famous people, you might never learn it at all.

I know what you're thinking. I know I'm an ex-con, but think about it. I was stripped of everything and confined. I did it. I self regulated. No poor me, no siree. I kept myself on a tight rein. I had to. I couldn't trust myself. Some people are born with it, some have their parent's example, and others enter the military. Some people learn it the hard way in prison, like me.

I didn't stop learning in prison and my confinement in prison polished my skills. I kept my body under control. Physically I worked hard, my body was fit. Mentally, I read every chance I got; I kept it sharp and tried to pay attention. Spiritually I fed my passions when I could. I fished, read, watch my pathetic wrestling and foremost enjoyed my kids. Emotionally I tried to keep it together, that was never my strong card anyway and I was pushed to the limit practically every day.

Mental regulation was my strong card. I watched what I fed my mind. I kept it on the fine things, the basics and true. Generally, in solitary I learned books gave me the friends I was not allowed. That held true in my marriage too. Books became my friends and took me to places I had always dreamed of seeing.

Once in awhile a friend would slip through the cracks. This was true of Louie. The Missus never found out about him. He was my friend at the old folk's home where I worked. He lived there not because he was old but due to the fact he was deformed. His parents had dropped him off. He had a normal head but a body of an infant. He wore diapers and everything. His head was fine and packed full of all the things that I enjoyed. He was always ready for a discussion of work on the Egyptian pyramids, or what it would be like working on a tuna boat. We argued over the Mayan ruins and the Great Wall of China. We both had a drooling desire to see the Seven Wonders of the World. Between discussions we would have checker play offs. He could push the checkers with a tongue depressor. I saw him nearly every day during coffee breaks. He was in a physical prison and I was in an emotional one. We understood each other.

My daughter met him and listened to our global arguments. She sat on the floor coloring in her book he bought her on the Seven Wonders of the World. Some times I'd be in a bind and Louis would just give me a wink and watch her for me. She played with him like a doll, combing his hair and such. He didn't seem to mind. She was always real careful with him, he was very delicate. Once I had to work late and I had left them together quite a while. When I got to his room, there they were. He was sleeping in his iron crib and she was curled in there right next to him with her

Chatty Cathy doll between then. She was always asking to take him home. Of all the dreams I had, I have to admit I would have loved to take him home. He would have been a good companion. It was just we did not have a home to take him to, just a house.

Louie was my best friend for maybe a good ten years. Then he caught the pneumonia and died. A new orderly had taken up his care, one who didn't have the patience for him. I heard him boasting about giving him a cold shower and leaving the window open all night on him. You know you can't do that to a baby. That orderly was just one of those prick workers who want a paycheck with the least resistance possible. It broke my heart to lose that friend. I missed Louis; he wasn't the sort of guy you could easily forget. There was a big hole in my life without him. But I was never the sort to fight over a dead body.

Trouble was this event with Louie went down right sour with the nursing staff . He was a man with many friends. For anyone being with him was like standing in the sunshine, he sparkled. He was popular. Those nurses let me know they were in the mood to hunt a little bear. Revenge. I was only ever interested in it once but it does one good to be presented with it. I wasn't one to pass it up. One nurse called me on the laundry line and said she had a gift arriving in chute five.

Yep, I opened the door and there that orderly lay in the laundry bin. Right drugged up he was. They had managed to drug him up and drag him over to the chute and let him free fall to me. I had to admire their effort. He was unconscious but he had survived the fall. I knew what I wanted. I padded him in dirty laundry and did to him what I saw many a screw do to an inmate in the big house. Nah, I didn't kill him. He wasn't worth it. Yet, he wouldn't be feeling right fine for a while either. When I finished I locked the door behind me.

Don't you know a funny thing happened, sometime in the middle of the night he woke up. He started screaming and a patient complained of noise coming from the chute. Ah, how sad. He had fallen into the chute all liquored up and was quite banged up. He was off for quite a spell and came back to do rehabilitation right there at the old folk's home, with those same nurses. Definitely not my cup of tea.

I only saw him once after that. I went up to his room, the room that had been Louie's. I had a little man to man talk with him. He decided it was in his best interest to put in for a transfer. He had worn out his welcome.

Maybe good old Louie wouldn't have lived much longer, but either way he didn't deserve what he got. I had the opportunity to straighten up the score, I did it for Louie.

Chapter 26

Eight Ball

I know, you don't have to tell me. I have a machine gun laugh, and I don't really care. I have used my laugh well and mainly at myself. I laugh at any thing at any time. See in this photograph, all my kids are laughing at me too. My oldest boy's head had the biggest smile, see here how it looks like half his head will fall off.

Yep, I hardly took any thing seriously after I got out of solitary. Not much seemed all that serious when compared to that. Especially my house. Every day when I entered that beast I would yell out at the top of my lungs "Home Sweet Home." I did it just for the hell of it and just because it never would be. My kid's knew what I meant and they'd come running. Other times I'd give them a sly smile and off we'd go taunting the Dragon's tale.

One day we went into high performance over grub. I don't have a clue what pocessed us. I threw those kids a look at the dinner table and we were off. I took a stab at the roast, if you could call it that, like an English lord. I made a rancid comment about it coming off a car tire the day before. We all started chewing and chewing. Then I took out my false teeth and set them by my plate. I made a comment about gumming it so as not to wreck my clackers. The kids got all worked up and really put on an act. It was exceedingly tough anyway.

My daughter picked up the pace and like a queen she stuck her fork into a boiling potato that was customarily baked in our kitchen. She pulled out all the grainy guts about two feet in the air. She added a remark that it was sad we were not the quality of people who knew the difference between a baking potato and a boiling potato.

My boy didn't want to be left behind and piped in her never minded the stale taste of watered down milk. Adding it had a unique taste when belched in classroom. He added it gave an added edge in getting through crowds.

The little guy chimed in he enjoyed the lumps in the gravy, it reminded him of cow snots. With this the Missus turned green. She was taking us seriously.

I won the competition comparing the tapioca to fish eyes. This demented banter paid off. It got us better grub, and gave us an insight to her mentality. We hardly could control our snickering.

Other times to lift the mood we'd all watch cartoons, or even Laurel and Hardy. I always enjoyed them in the picture show "Swiss Miss" with that ape on the swing bridge. Apes are my weakness. It always made our lives seem not that bad. After cartoons we'd stoop to rubber band wars or some such nonsense.

Of course my kids were the brunt of some of my jokes. I never wanted them to get a big head. Some times I'd line 'em up and swagger back and forth looking at them. I'd mutter about having a lot of things wrong with me and being eight ball and all. Then

I'd point to them and say they all had one thing wrong with them that I never would. I whisper real low, "Your mother's blood."

Holy Cow. I didn't think they would take it all so serious. The first time they all broke down and cried. After I worked on them awhile they caught on. They got me back plenty too. They'd hide my cigarettes before we went out fishing just to watch me see snakes. Then when I couldn't take any more I'd make a ballerina leap out of the boat on shore. I'd scurry up the shore to buy a pack. They'd trick me into eating sour candy which I couldn't abide but always fell for. I'd peel down the car window and spit it out fifty feet in the air. I never leaned my lesson on that one.

We all worked out a routine for church going. If the Missus got up early we'd sleep in and vice versa. Then we'd head on out to the Cathedral without her. The kids would hide me under a pew so I could catch up on some sleep and poke me if I started snoring too loud. Then we'd all march out all pious just in case the Missus had sent any spies.

Once things didn't go according to plan. We were almost in the front, not a good choice for sleep. I nodded off so fast that I was still kneeling and holding my head just right with my hands. I was the epitome of pious before I started snoring. Then I guess I squeaked out a pop corn fart. That sent my kids into uncontrolled laughter. They hid down in the pew. It looked like I was alone from the back. The bishop in the pulpit had the real view looking down on the whole mess.

I built up to a nice crescendo snoring and I guess on the downside I was smacking my flannel mouth like an old horse waiting for the glue factory. This scenario see sawed back and forth a while, till the competition was too much for the bishop and he halted his sermon. All I knew was that something was wedged in my behind at that point and I started wiggling against it. I got off balance and my head cracked against the pew like a cannon. I shook myself awake and pulled my kids foot out of my ass. I looked around and holy hell all two or three hundred people were looking at my scrawny self. Then I look up to the bishop and realized that his mouth was closed for once.

I just gruntally stood up and said half awake, "Jesus Christ, kid's let's get the hell out of here." My kids in hiding, now stood up with me and we made our humbled way out of there. I learned a valuable lesson that day. If you are going to sleep in church keep to the back where the drunks are. It's safer.

Chapter 27

Launch

Laughter is the best policy. As long as we are on this subject, I need to fess up to another mess. You'll probably find out about it either way.

My youngest got me to laugh and shit my pants at the same time. He turned out to be a fearless kid. I didn't fully understand this until he hit four years of age. We both fell sick with the same fever of sorts. Kites. We started out with our pathetic homemade paper jobs. We made them up in the basement during the week, so we could bust them up on the weekend. I even had fishing reels to reel them in. It was a good operation.

Then, for some ungodly reason we walked past a toy store window. There we were introduced to the new love of our lives, the Black Bat. This monster had a six-foot wingspan and an ominous thick plastic coat. Both of us just stopped dead in out tracks and began salivating. What can I say? We got the thing up and running for the weekend. It turned out to be a fine spring blue day with popcorn clouds. This kite happened to be a bigger operation than planned. We hauled it over to the vacant school playground. I walked the kite back; it was too big for my kids to wrangle. My girl was point man and my oldest boy was rope handler. Or, that was the way it was supposed to go. I did not see the altercation break out. I was busy concentrating on launch. A gust blew and wham out of my arms it wrenched. Then I noticed my oldest boy on the ground and writhing in pain, obviously the victim of my youngest's orthopedic shoes. My daughter was off at a good clip running after the kite.

Yep, that is when I glanced up and spotted my youngest sky bound. I would have shat my pants right there if I had the time. I threw the keys to the seven year old and told him to follow us with the car. He was perfectly qualified to do this and his ears prickled with the opportunity of a lifetime. I tore off after the kite, now a block away. I caught up with my daughter just in time to see the kite nearing the power lines. Thank God an updraft caught it and I saw my son whipped around and back again.

Off we went back towards the school in time to see the kite disappear over the school building and my youngest passed out of sight. We found him dangling by his suspenders in the big spruce on the side of the brick building. I shimmied up and passed him down to his sister. I back tracked and grabbed the keys out of the Chevy, as my oldest son had decided to park on the school lawn. Holy Hell!

I raced back to examine the youngest but he was all ready for another go with nary a scratch. I was a lucky man. I even found the kite a few days later on the roof of the school. Moral of the story, do not buy a kite bigger than the size of your kid.

My oldest boy got me the best when he was almost grown. No, it was not the time when I got myself wedged under the Chevy like a blowfish. I don't consider that his best work.

This was the time we were out ice fishing. My boy had gotten disgustedly bored after watching me sleep in the bunk for thirty odd hours. He must have been contemplating the old geezer on the tractor pulling the icehouses off the lake with chains. It was getting end of season. The light bulb must have gone off in that brain. I can't blame him. He pounced.

"Dad, wake up! We're going to die. The ice houses are blowing away."

Up I go. I take a quick gander. Right as rain, the icehouse is moving. From my perspective I cannot see the old geezer pulling it off. We leap into the car. Off we go and once again leave all our gear. I did not get a good look until we were to the highway. There I spotted the geezer on the tractor. I had to admit, he got me good.

My daughter's humor is much more subtle. I'll give you an example of a more glowing moment. I called her apartment to complain about being in another car accident. She dryly listened once again to the litany for a spell. I explained how the Missus never looked when I asked her if anyone was coming on the right. She never looked, just said all clear. You can imagine the rest.

She said, "Dad if your lips are still moving you're not that hurt." Nope, I never could fool that kid. She went on to explain, that if I insisted on driving with the Missus it was tantamount to suicide. If I was serious about suicide, I should make better plans.

She explained how the house was the most excellent place to go out properly. That I should position myself, so that brain matter would hit three kitchen walls and ceiling. The recoil would propel my body down the basement stairs and leave excellent carnage in its wake. This would make most body parts per square inch to clean.

Now that was good. I chewed on that one quite awhile and called her back to congratulate her on that one. That, and the fact I was swearing off driving with the Missus completely.

Chapter 28

Mutiny

Even I know I shouldn't fall asleep in church. It ain't a good thing, and you must never leave halfway through. What can I say? There is no excuse for the likes of me. I know now that God always saw right through the likes of me.

Then again, God can see right though the likes of religion. It has a lot to answer for. Most all wars have been carried out in the guise of God's good name. I bet he really enjoys that. Think about all the body mutilations, human sacrifice, stoning not to mention the mindless haughty and prejudiced attitudes. He must get exhausted listening to the mindless incessant repetitive praying. It must sound like a bunch of bees in his head. I think the closer to God you get, the more you close your mouth. At least in my case the closest I felt to God was out on a lake with my mouth shut. I could just sit and enjoy the beautiful painting before me, one that continuously changed. I could just sit and listen to God and feel his breeze on my bones.

It just seemed that I was given a life and needed to go and do just that. I didn't want to be weak and let someone else with another agenda tell me how to conduct myself. They didn't have all the facts. Christ in his day didn't put much stock in religious leaders. He went about telling them off right, left and center too. He wasn't at temple everyday with his nose stuck in a scroll. He was a regular type of guy with his own set of problems.

I have met many a so called religious man I could not trust to turn my back on. I have met men in the big house that never set a foot in church. I could have entrusted my kids with some of them in full confidence. There I was in the belly of the beast, so to speak, with one big fat religious Missus. She was the mother of my children. Yet, I could not turn my back to her. I could not trust her with our own children.

I did it all as far as religion is concerned. I sat in on many a religious ceremony, Catholic as you know, Baptist, Protestant and even those scary snake twirlers. I even happened on a black Pentecostal born again tent revival. We were all kneeing and one by one they started confessing their sins. I was getting a might itchy, knowing my turn was coming up. Where would I start, and could I ever end? Then when my number came up I just piped in "I pass." What the hell else could I do?

I thought they would run me out on a rail with that comment, and me being the wrong color and all. As it turned out I got an invitation to one of the best barbeques of my life. It could have been one of the best in all my history. Everyone was right nice but kept the kids a might out of my reach. I didn't feel bad, they were just using caution. I was the fly in the milk so to speak. I met a right fine man called Ralph. He was a bit down on his luck. I felt for him being married, with a baby to boot. I told him to come around the shit factory. It wasn't good work but it would do.

He did too and was a might fine worker. He learned the ropes. I taught him everything I could. He even stopped by the house with his wife and baby with a gift for helping him through his bad patch. My Missus got acting right nasty about that one. She said nothing in front of them but, I got the lecture of a life time when they left. In no uncertain terms, she made it known a bullet waited for them, and then for me if they ever returned. Our house was just too holy a place for the likes of any of them, as far as my wife was concerned. I mentioned my predicament to Ralph and he understood. We met away from the house and my kids came with. He was a real friend. Ralph was better than the likes of us, and I encouraged him to move on and get his own business up and running. He was capable, with a very supportive wife. He had better circumstance than me.

This same volcano blew years later again. My daughter was going to be picked up for church by a black family. My Missus barred herself in front of the door. My daughter nimbly ran out the kitchen door and told them to gun the car. My daughter got the same lecture when she got home. My Missus ugly underside was revealed again. It set into motion a full fledged mutiny.

The next week my daughter had had it. She flatly refused to go to church at all. This altercation took place down stairs in my daughter's so called room. My daughter got worked over real good, but she never made a sound. My Missus marched her pious self upstairs and started in on me. Yep, our daughter was going to hell in a hand basket. She was now rebellious as well as a heathen. She'd be pregnant in no time flat. On and on it went, I got up out of a dead sleep for this?

I barreled down those stairs quick for a confrontation. There stood my girl. She had heard the racket and was waiting. My daughter confirmed that she was refusing to go. She quietly said she had enough of the hypocrisy. She just asked one thing before her punishment. I agreed and she took off her blouse and stood there with just her bra on. I stood stunned, not a scratch was on her arms or face this time. Her ribs and kidneys had taken the brunt and I saw she was having trouble moving. I helped put her blouse back on, real slow like not to hurt her. I had tears in my eyes and what can you say?

Bam! My veins went white hot. I got my steam up marching up those stairs. My Missus must have smelt it wasn't going her way. She ran around pulling down the window shades. My boys tumbled out and cheered me on. I ranted, kicked walls, slammed doors and threw a few plates for punctuation. I could not believe she could go this far while I had been asleep. What more was this woman capable of? Then we all took a vote. I said we all lived in the United States of American and so far it was still a free country. I had everyone raise their hands, who was in favor of religious freedom. My daughter was still down stairs but I didn't want her to vote. I didn't need it. The boys and I were the majority.

No one in my family would ever be forced into a church any longer. My boys were cheering and jumping up and down. Out poured the stories of all the Sundays they hid out in snow banks or in the woods rather than be confined in church. They enthusiastically related how they would enter the church in one door, with the Missus following them with the car behind them. Then, they would run out the other side and ditch the service. They made sure they shook off the communist spy tailing them.

This was a huge hit for my Missus. I knew there would be a price to pay and it likely would land on my daughter head. I went back down stairs and explained things. I spoke softly as not to be heard by "Bat Ears" on the stair landing. We would need to take precaution. I explained this was a battle won, but the war was far from over.

Chapter 29

Aces

It's one thing to discipline yourself, to keep yourself in check. Now, I found myself rattled to discipline my kids. I'm the first to admit I am an emotional midget. I had to get it done all the same. Here I was saddled with a wife that would keep us awake all night, sleep all day and nag in between. Her normal attire was fifteen year old pajamas. So that's what greeted me when I walked in the door. A frazzled nut wearing pajamas.

I started early on, getting it into my kid's heads, that she was their mother and to show respect. It was necessary just treat her as if she was sick. I wanted them to learn from the cockroach and skirt around things. I tired to keep the pot from boiling over as much as possible.

There was no sense to waste time on something so dark and negative. What is the point? My hope was with my kids to grow and spread their wings. Most kids learn discipline by example. I was fortunate to have kids that listened most of the time. I usually gave them one warning and after that I spoke no more. Kids don't listen if you repeat yourself. I was the Dad and I had all the aces.

Now take the bicycle incident. I warned them not to park their bikes behind my car in the driveway. When I left for work I had no time to waste rearranging them. I politely asked the first time. The lunk heads didn't listen. Next I gave them a full blown warning. Yep you guessed it, the next day I backed over the whole lot. Funny thing, I never had the slightest problem after that. I never had to open my trap again.

Now hair cuts were problematic. The Missus would start the haircutting right during wrestling. So I had wresting in two rooms at once. I'd be heavily concentrating and getting all worked up with the match. She'd be screaming at a wiggling kid in the kitchen. Then wrestling would be going full bore. Then a kid was screaming. Lovely. Here we go in stereo.

Usually I made it into the kitchen during the commercials. Finally the day came when I wove the white flag. Wrestling was finished and so was I. The '56 Chevy was fired up and the boys in the back seat. I smugly went to the barber. When we arrived back home they stayed put in the car for quite awhile. Things hadn't quite gone in their favor. They were the next best thing to bald and I had carved out a slice of peace and quiet for a few months regarding the issue. Not bad.

When the Missus was just out for blood like a gladiator, it wasn't a problem. I'd take the boys downstairs with a huge belt. We had a good routine going. I'd be yelling and throwing things around. I'd slap the wall with my belt and a kid would respond with an appropriate scream. We were just like that hokey pokey wrestling on television.

Till my daughter quietly slipped downstairs with the Missus prodding. We all were stunned, like moose in the headlights. I gave the signal to keep going, and the sign for her to keep her yap shut. After a time, she moseyed upstairs. She was good, she never ratted on us.

The day did arrive when major discipline was necessary. The boys were in fancy private high school and messing up. All my hard earned money was going into bankruptcy again. So if they were going to act like criminals, they could live like criminals. Surprise! I tooted them off for the obligatory prison hair cut. They got home to find their clothes were gone except what was necessary, one change. They had one pair of high top tennis shoes and that got them though the winter. They had some high stepping to do and they'd better make it fast or freeze. I refused to squander more money on private school. They were enrolled in night classes and were expected to work during the day. No more time on their hands for the likes of them.

They did beautifully after the sulk wore off. The youngest boy excelled at engineering and the oldest boy started working with catering which has given him a nice living for over twenty years.

It is a father's responsibility to get your child what he needs to get out of the nest and fly. Easy or hard mine did.

Chapter 30

Blue Haze

Now I will belly up to the table and relate how I ended up in the big house. I was seventeen and in puppy love. I'll admit I was a hot head. We were in love and we wanted a future together. Both parents thought this was a bad idea. They both had the same plan.

My father was the town attorney. He worked me over quite well. He slit my head open right nice and locked me out in the cold South Dakota winter night. I had a hunch the same would happen to her. Only she was worked over to a nasty degree. Her father was the sheriff. I know we were both young and on a slippery slope. Still touching a woman like that never sat well with me.

I laid in wait in the barn for that devil. He must have been informed. He was packing heat. I didn't care. I met him head on man to man. When the weapon was pulled on me I took it clean out of his hand. I did to him what he did to his daughter, and made damn sure his wife and daughter would never have to fear him again. I set them free.

Did I shoot him? I probably should have put him out of his misery but I got too worked up. I don't know why to this day I didn't. I did leave him with no chance of a full recovery. I know it was wrong. I could have got "Old Sparky" but instead I got seventeen years.

I probably would have got sprung sooner if I hadn't shown such poor behavior in prison. That cost me two years in solitary. I already explained I poured scalding soap on a screw. I did that so I could work on the chain gang outside. But that is only partially true.

It was also a plain case of revenge for my buddy Smokey Joe. That guard had scalded my buddy in the shower after refusing his sexual advances. My buddy never recovered, that cost my friend his life. I evened the score when I was presented with a golden opportunity. Yep, it cost me two years but I made damn sure that guard was not capable of buggering anyone again. I had good aim with that boiling laundry soap.

It happened the same way with that China man. I could not let that bastard pick on that poor man and get away with it. It don't sit right with me.

As long as it is true confessions, I'll fess up to one more indiscrete event. But only one. Later in life, I was working at the parking lot. I must have been pushing sixty. I was just whistling my guts out and mopping out the elevator just before closing up. I must have been pretty loud, and with my ass hanging out and all.

Bam, two men jumped me from behind. They knew what they were doing. The cash register was full from the night's take. One gun was pointed at my head and the other in my ribs. They thought they had an easy target, withered old man with a messed up back and lame foot.

I let out a sorry sigh. Here we go again. I kicked the one behind me right in the nuts like a jack hammer. I spun and caught the other with the mop handle up against the wall till his feet were dangling off the ground. It was a perfect choke hold.

I guess I might have gone a little over board given such an opportunity. When I finished, I just locked them in the elevator. I hauled myself over to the ticket booth to call the cops. That's when I spied the patrol sitting across the street. I do believe most cops aren't lazy but these two happened to be. They had seen the whole thing and were too afraid to intervene. I guess to them it would have been no big deal to have one less old fart on the planet.

Thank Christ those bastards had picked on me. They would not be capable of doing it again. It hadn't gone the way the coppers planed. Some times the line between cop and criminal is real fuzzy.

The ambulance came and I finished moping out the elevator with all the blood. The cops wanted a full report taken in the squad. Fine. I gave my report to those cowards in that squad and it worked out right fine anyway. I had just finished off a fine plate of beans before the incident. I was feeling pretty ripe. I just sat and fired off some silent gas till the air was filled with a fine blue haze. They let go of me right quick.

I bailed out and just looked up at the starry sky and watched my breath escape in the cold night air. I was still breathing. I had survived again like a cat with nine lives.

Chapter 31

Smoke Rings

I have to admit looking back I was a very lucky man. You might think all the time I spent in the big house combined with solitary ain't that lucky. Then to top it off add another fifty years with the Missus. That was no cake walk. Yet it did not conquer me.

I made poor choices early on and I paid for those choices. I stayed the course so to speak. Since I didn't ride "Old Sparky", I experienced passion and love. I trained my mind, body and spirit. I never shifted from work and I enjoyed my leisure. I enjoyed good grub when I got it and I knew how to go without. I kept clean and organized inside my body and out. With the eight years of education and the years God gave, I tried to cover all my bases.

I knew the compassion of the willow. I experienced all sorts of pain. I tried to be honest without letting the cat out of the bag. I saddled up to humility and kissed humiliation. I had the ability to laugh, most of the time at myself. I loved a good piece of conversation and never passed up a piece of solitude.

When good old cancer saddled up to me, I thought it was my enemy. After eight years with it, I enjoyed the down time and solitude. I got my chance to think about myself.

I would not have gotten this time had my Missus not made a fateful move. After over twenty years of not having contact with my daughter, the Missus made the phone call. Yep, she thought the drama could begin long distance. My daughter had already been headed off at the pass by her brother. She had called the hospital and had a nice cozy chat with the nurse in charge of my case. Both being nurses, they had a confab of sorts. I not only had cancer but my blood tests showed the medication that I should have been getting was not there at all. Yet, other sundry items were there in abundance. The Missus was playing fast and loose with my life. How was I to know? Now that I had cancer I guess I was ready to be thrown onto the dog pile. Used up.

That was some phone call. I don't rightly know what was said. I wasn't privy to the conversation. The Missus kept a real low tone like a cornered rat. I over heard my Missus agreeing that we were all adults. No, my daughter would not need to come up. Yes, God was not blind. That was about all my ears peeled off. After that the Missus let out a gasp. That was the only time I ever can remember my Missus with her trap shut on the phone. It didn't go the way the Missus had planned. My daughter could see through what ever was going on. She certainly wasn't buying what the Missus was up to. Maybe the Missus was fixing on vampiring my daughter's neck as soon as she could get me gone.

Things took a big turn for the better with good old cancer. At first it kind of just crept up on me. I did a lot of looking back on my lot in life. I never amounted to much as far as material things were concerned. I could always pack all my personals in a small satchel. What I'm talking about are my opportunities with my kids. They survived and stood on their own. The Chinaman got to see his kids grow and get married too. I married the Missus and gave her a project that for the most part kept her off the streets. Old Bessie and the laundry girls had a better life. I always could look back on my time with Carey and know we had the sense not to throw a monkey wrench in our path. For better or worse, when I was presented with revenge I took it.

That's how I lived another eight years. They had given me six months, can you believe that? I had good care. The Missus made sure of that. The tables were turned. I was surrounded by my favorite things, books and my new addiction that television show "Divorce Court." Nope, I never got tired of that one. I could dream right? I hated to stoop that low, but I got addicted like. I finally got a chance to rest. I took vacations with my mind whether it was the drugs or not I don't know. I even felt like I got stuck by a bolt of blue lightening and talked to my daughter about it. She told me not to worry.

I wish that doctor had been a gambling man. He gave me one hundred eighty days and my body squeezed out almost three thousand. Yep, that was quite a wrestling match with good old cancer. Can you imagine me dying of natural causes?

Chapter 32

Blue Skies

Go on, you can say it. I ain't a religious man, never had the time really. Mainly I hate the hypocrisy. I never stopped anyone going full bore for it either. I've seen it bolster the ego of many a man, and not for the better. I think it can get in the way of who God really is. Religion has a lot to answer for.

As for me, I learned more about God out on a lake though my tears than listening to a stuffy hypocrite tell me off from a pulpit. I tried to listen real quiet to what He had to tell me about my life. I tried to keep my trap shut.

That don't mean I didn't try the lot. I seen the snake charmers get bit. The Lutherans weren't ready for the likes of me. I got a dose of Mormon logic with Carey's husband. I did like the Baptist's music but in the finish let's face it, I ain't black. Pentecostals getting the spirit makes me a mite edgy. My daughter's husband was a slimy Witness elder that couldn't keep his pant's zipper up. I need not go into the Catholics, you know my history there.

For me most everything in life is attitude. I guess you could say it is my religion. I did what I had to do and I met it full on. I tried to train my mind to the positive side. That is all I had to give the people around me, mainly my kids.

That is why I took them out in a boat as much as I did. They had a chance to see God's handiwork up close and enjoy the peace and quiet. You might not make the world peaceful but you can give it to you family as much as possible.

I always hoped my kids would not be addicted to drama. I didn't want them to inherit that from the Missus if at all possible, and for the most part they were not. Once in a while it creeps up on you anyway.

My daughter was hit right between the eyes with it. That kid was cursed with my miserable luck. She was seventeen and her beau Michael was sent to Vietnam. They were sweet hearts. I loved to watch them on the swing out back holding hands. You couldn't help admit what they had was strong. He was from a good Irish family and raised well. He never minded the Missus and could stand his ground with her if cornered. A definite plus he would need. I watched them roller skating a time or two and it was like watching one body. They were so synchronized in their movements.

The funniest thing was he understood my kid, and how he did, I don't know. I never seen them talk much; it was like some type of telepathy or something. What they had I can't rightly explain. Once he left for the war, it didn't take long before we got the news he wouldn't be coming back.

My daughter never wore color after that and her whole being slumped. She had a strong and deep love for that boy. I tried hard to pull her back. Finally, I took her out for dinner, just her and me.

I was trolling around for conversation. I wanted to grab anything I could from those dark algae depths of despair. She raised her eyes and looked at me square on and asked if I had ever been in love.

So I debased myself right then and there. I crossed that parent line and told her about my love and loss. Man to man. I related my ill fated love and my true feelings. I also told her, at the end of the day, I knew Carey. I knew she would want the best for me. She would want to see me whole and happy. I related that it was Carey that got me through every dark day. That, whether I never saw her again, my life was better off for knowing her. I had loved and been loved. I would never want to erase that, no matter how bad the ache was. If there was another side after death, I'd love to meet up to her and say "Howdy do" and tip my hat.

I looked straight at my daughter and spoke with a dry eye. I had not opened my mouth about Carey in over twenty odd years. It took a lot. What I said was true and hard. I can still feel it cut like a knife.

We sat there quite a spell after that. My daughter's shoulders squared off a bit. I could see her breathing low and slow. It was like an essence was being poured back into her. I hoped she would get back into her skin.

Not long after that I was happily surprised. We had to cart my oldest boy off to the hospital with an allergy attack. He kept blaming his sister for it. Whatever he did I'm sure he deserved it. He had a loathsome way of irritating her. Now I don't know what she used on him but it got him good. The best part for me was knowing she was fighting back. She was in her skin again.

Chapter 33

Harbor Lights

I did a crazy thing when I turned sixty two. I took stock of my life and talked to an advisor about my retirement. I got my money put back in my name. Then I took a year off. I put my satchel in my little orange Toyota Pick Up. I bought an orange one so I wouldn't lose it in the parking lot. I didn't want the police thinking I was daft in the head. Then I looked up at those fine cotton clouds and started driving.

I took my time and headed through the Black Hills near where I grew up, then passed old Mount Rushmore at my leisure. Montana was next and I visited my cousins. The Grand Canyon was a nice slice of pie. Las Vegas with all the racket and lights made me a mite edgy. California and the desert felt good on my bones. I wasn't sure what my daughter would think when I knocked on her door in Palm Springs. You know, would she be embarrassed by the likes of me. I didn't want to get in her way.

It was just fine. She had a spare bedroom. I wasn't intending to say, just to pass through. Something way down deep snapped in me. Peace and quiet. I hit that bed with those clean sheets. I smelled the night air, heard the coyotes in the distance and looked up at the navy blue night sky. I slept. I woke up about six weeks later or so. My daughter had thought I was dead a few times and poked me awake just to make sure. Then one day I sat straight up and scratched my head. I decided it was time I had a smoke and went outside.

Bam. Just like that, it hit me. There was a swimming pool. I fired myself up and swam around the better part of the next two weeks. If I wasn't in the pool, you could sneak around the side and find me in my new luxury, the Jacuzzi. Hell, who ever invented that should be given a medal. The next thing you know, I was playing pool with some of those other old farts I met. They had the solution for my bum knee, yep, good old WD40. What ever that stuff has in it healed my bum knee in no time flat. I had lost interest in smoking with that crackle dry air. I always was under the impression Palm Springs was the elephant graveyard for humans. Now could see why. My nerves simmered down and my veins disappeared. I felt like a million bucks. Not a bad way to die.

I even got me a job at the Circle K store to give my daughter space. I never missed a meal though, it was my daughter was cooking. I couldn't help it. I took advantage. On our days off we flitted around like those beautiful hummingbirds. We hiked Palm Canyon. Once a ram, bold as brass, jumped right in front of us. I nearly shat my pants. I saw the ocean for the first time in San Diego. It was just too immense to contemplate. I had to stand and scratch my head awhile. Next thing you know I was signed up on the fishing boat and I didn't even care if I caught a thing. The song "Harbor Lights" took on a whole new meaning.

See this photograph? I am at Disneyland. I thought it was only for kids but what the hell. It was entertaining. I got on every ride. I didn't care what those kids thought, let them laugh. Dumbo,

Peter Pan and the Pirates in that boat, well what can I say? The train ride though the Grand Canyon during a lightening storm, I did it all, and even the haunted house. After life in my house, I could have given them a few tips on that one. I drank a Mint Julep for the first time and even bought me some mouse ears. I fell asleep in the back seat on the way home with the rest of the kids. So what.

Some days we headed on up to Idyllwild to throw snow balls at each other. We'd throw our books in the car and read out by Hemet Lake. Seeing those trout jumping around made me salivate. I waltzed around a few date shakes. It's a funny thing how much time I spent in the water in the desert. How I sat in that Jacuzzi. I looked up at those snow capped lavender mountains. I could smell the orange blossoms. I did it all at the same time. It sure beat shoveling snow out of the drive.

That is how a year snuck by. I could have stayed there forever. I told my daughter just that. In the finish, I had to leave the peace of the Wild West. My conscience would not let me rest. My youngest still needed tending to. He was never very strong. You want to hear a good one? To save face, my wife had spread around I had died. Ain't that a good one? Sounds just like her, don't it?

Chapter 34

Blue Velvet

Are you back again? Sooner or later your going to have to ask yourself just why you're hanging around. Oh well, what's the difference. You've kind of grown on me. I've enjoyed these evenings, just shooting the breeze. I've never talked so much in my life.

Now looking back on my life, you could say he got what he deserved. It's true, I guess. At any rate, it is a lot more than I expected. I always said I was never afraid of Hell after being married to the Missus and that's the honest to God's truth. Time in the Big House was preferable to that. After all is said and done, I never wanted to believe the one upstairs was a narrow minded, racist priss. Every minute I spent out on a lake told me the opposite. In a lot of ways, it's like you get what you believe in. That can be Hell in itself. Be careful what you wish for. That is all I'll say about that.

I always put stock into what good old Mark Twain said. Like him, "I'll take heaven for the climate and Hell for the companionship." When I did come over to this side, it was a relief. Yea, I watched that whole funeral deal. Smorgasbord with my dead body in the room, ain't my idea of fun. Oh well, what the Hell do I know? After that, I did just a bit of reflection on things. I got to see myself and my kids from a whole new point of view. I was shown all we had endured as children and as adults. You might think that's stupid, but everyone has their likes and dislikes. Even that so called Jesus Christ is interested in humans.

I did a bit of roaming too. I had a chance to see a bit of what I had always been reading about. It felt good to stay around the earth. Then, my youngest joined me over here about five years after I left. He died of the same damn thing, can you believe that? It took him much quicker though. He's doing a lot better on this side. He's been working on a place for himself. He wants a real home. I mosey over and give him a hand now and then. He's at peace now and understands it.

When a real job opening came up, I jumped on it. I was never a slacker any way. I put in my two cents about why I was right for the job. Hot damn, if I didn't get it. I got the assignment.

It's only fair. My daughter saved her brothers lives and added quite a few years to mine. There is a whole heard of people she has added time to. Now it's her turn. That's why I'm hanging around here. I never minded the California climate in the least, so that's a bonus. My daughter finally found her love late in life, only to lose him so suddenly. Then, with all the rest that happened, we really weren't sure she would pull through. It was decided that it was in her best interest that a guardian be appointed.

That's, my job now, just like before. I give her reason to go on. I leave her pennies just like I used to do. I tell her stories at night and make her laugh in her sleep. I give her great ideas when she stands in front of that ironing board. I watch out for her. I just have to be careful she doesn't smell my cigarettes. That always irritated her to no end. She has the nose of a blood hound.

Him? He comes around almost every evening. He loved my daughter very much. You've seen him before. I kind of distract him like, so my daughter can sleep. I play him a mean game of chess. Some times we switch and play cribbage, just about anything to take his mind off. I gently explain things to him. Mainly I just out and out sidetrack him. Poor bastard, but he's getting better. How? Crushed to death he was, far before his time. But that is his story to tell. I ain't spilling no beans on that subject. He can tell it when he has a mind to.

I'll probably hang around as long as it takes here and then move on. I'd like to meet up with a few of my old buddies. I'd really like to see one person in particular. I have my request in. I'm getting ready.

Yep, like I said I'm a guardian. Can you believe it? I'll turn around a wee bit so you can take a gander. See them, they are my wings. There not the souped up version. I'm not ready for that yet. I'm just going to take things real easy and slow. Aren't they nice? My favorite color of blue and smooth as velvet.